SHORT STORY INTERNATIONAL

Tales by the World's Great Contemporary Writers Presented Unabridged

All selections in
Short Story International
are published full and
unabridged.

Editor
Sylvia Tankel

Associate Editor
Erik Sandberg-Diment

Contributing Editor
John Harr

Assistant Editors
Mildred Butterworth
Debbie Kaufman
Kirsten Hammerle

Art Director
Charles J. Berger

Circulation Director
Nat Raboy

Production Director
Michael Jeffries

Business Manager
John O'Connor

Publisher
Sam Tankel

Volume 14, Number 83, December 1990.
Short Story International (USPS 375-970)
Copyright © by International Cultural
Exchange 1990. Printed in U.S.A. All rights
reserved. Reproduction in whole or in part
prohibited. Second-class postage paid at
Great Neck, N.Y. 11022 and at additional
mailing offices. **Editorial offices: P.O. Box
405, Great Neck, N.Y. 11022.** Enclose
stamped, self-addressed envelope with
submission. One year (six issues) subscription
for U.S., U.S. possessions $22, Canada $24
(US), other countries $25 (US). Single copy
price $4.95 (US). **For subscriptions and
address changes write to Short Story
International, P.O. Box 405, Great
Neck, N.Y. 11022.** *Short Story
International* is published bimonthly by
International Cultural Exchange, 6 Sheffield
Road, Great Neck, N.Y. 11021. Postmaster
please send Form 3579 to P.O. Box 405,
Great Neck, N.Y. 11022.

Table of Contents

(See page 157 for a special Holiday coupon.)

Copyrights
and acknowledgments

We wish to express deep thanks to the authors, publishers, translators and literary agents for their permission to publish the stories in this issue.

"First Chocolate Bar" by Graham Sheil. Copyright Graham Sheil. "The Vagabond" by Mary Drake appeared in *North Shore Times*. Copyright Mary Drake. "Spring Festival Eve" by Da Li appeared in *Chinese Literature,* 1985. Translation by Song Shouquan. By permission. "The Immigrants" by Naim Siddiqui, 1990. "Walls" by Amnon Shamosh appeared in *Midstream*. Translation by Nili Wachtel. Copyright Amnon Shamosh. "Delayed Homecoming" by Teruko Hyuga, 1990. "L'Italiana" by Francis Ebejer, 1990. "A Clear Day in May" from *Noveller i utvalg* by Johan Borgen. Copyright 1961. Published by Gyldendal Norsk Forlag. Translation by Amanda Langemo, 1990. "The Exile" from *The God Stealer and Other Stories* by F. Sionil José. Published by R.P. Garcia Publishing Company. Copyright 1968 F. Sionil José. "Reception" from *The London Embassy* by Paul Theroux. Published by Houghton Mifflin Company, Boston. Copyright © 1983 Cape Cod Scriveners Company. Reprinted by permission of the publisher and Aitken & Stone Ltd. "Cookie" by Mignon Holland Anderson originally appeared in *The Maryland Review*. Copyright 1986 Mignon Holland Anderson. "Integration" by Uyen Loewald, 1990. "Door Handle" by Fadil Hadzich. Copyright Fadil Hadzich. English translation by Josip Novakovich, 1990.

Photo credits: Paul Theroux by Nancy Maguire.

"I saw my father's head sink lower and lower
until it was right against his knees. "

First Chocolate Bar

BY GRAHAM SHEIL

SPOTS and spillings across the stark-white tablecloth testified to a
meal that had been attacked and defeated. Dribbles of Burgundy
sauce, splashes of bouillabaisse, remnants of salad and brittle flakes
from crusts of bread and rolls told the tale that we'd done it royally.
There were three of us—two Australians, one German—business-
class passengers grounded by a dispute between the airlines and
plane refuelers. Given vouchers for use in the airport cafeteria,
we'd stood staring at dried wrinkled skins on sausages and at
battered fish glistening with oil in the cafeteria warmers—then
opted to treat ourselves to the top-floor restaurant instead.

A waitress took away the cheese platter and plates, and brought
coffee and chocolate pralines.

Hans took one of the pralines, unwrapped it from its deep green
cellophane wrapping, then held the dark chocolate as though
unsure whether he'd eat it or not.

"I will tell you," he said, "of my first bar of chocolate."

Over oysters we'd quite heatedly disagreed about the strike (we two Australians backing the airlines, Hans tending toward sympathy for the refuelers); during the beefsteak and the bouillabaisse there was mournful agreement about the state of the dollar; over cheese, the depressing acknowledgment that continually expanding economies were gone forever. Coffee, and pralines, was certainly the time for something more mellow.

"What I really mean," Hans said, "is a chocolate bar—like a Mars Bar—with dark nougat or similar inside.

"During the war I'd had solid chocolate, not often, and then only when I was taken with other children away from the family home in a village, almost a suburb, out from Stuttgart.

"My father had had an optician's shop in that village. By standards of the time, his shop was very fine. A glass panel between shop and workshop allowed people to see him at work shaping lenses on a ceramic stone with a water drip. The shop itself was carpeted and there were private cubicles for his clients' selection of spectacle frames. Each cubicle had a wall mirror and a hand mirror, both edged in gold filigree.

"It was not that we were particularly wealthy or that the business was so thriving, rather it was my father's pride that he present his profession as one with a distinctive and distinguished heritage. 'Spinoza,' he often used to say, 'was also a shaper of lenses.'

"His attitude toward civic affairs showed similar pride. Once he had been burgomaster of our village. When corruption of councils took place under the Nazis, he resigned from the council, but remained on committees to do with preservation of buildings with distinctive architecture. Our village had narrow cobblestone streets with three-story buildings—often shop below, two stories of dwelling above—standing right against the edge of the footpath. The emblems of tradesmen hung out across the street from above shop doorways. These buildings, many two-, three-, some even four-hundred years old, all had wooden shutters and window boxes painted pink, always pink, under each dwelling window.

"Need I tell you my father's other great pride, beside his profession, was that his shop and our home was three-and-a-half centuries old with pink window boxes planted with tulips and narcissus?

"Twice during the war I was taken from this home to a children's camp in rural Saxony. The first time I was allowed home, there was no change to the village. I heard my mother and father speak of Allied bombing raids reaching further and further south.

"My second homecoming was after the war had ended. I was by then nine years old, and my village was changed, changed forever.

"Craters and hillocks of broken and charred paving stones barred the way where winding cobblestone streets had been. Buildings that had stood for two-, three-, four-hundred years, had become heaps of rubble, or they were fire-blackened shells, or holes in the ground where broken gas pipes and water pipes jutted up out of a sludge of mud and water.

"What had been my father's shop below, our home above, was now one of these holes.

"And my father...my father's pride, his whole sense of self-worth, had fallen with the fall of his home and shop.

"Without his optician's shop, no longer burgomaster or councillor, without the need ever again to serve on committees for the preservation of architecturally distinctive buildings, my father became in his own eyes little more than nothing.

"There was change of another kind in my mother. She had previously been an appendage, as it were, of my father: my father the optician, my father the burgomaster, my father the committeeman. Now my father's fall became the cause of my mother's rise. It was she who scoured the village to secure an only partially destroyed shop from where my father could again commence business, and it was she who bargained and begged to obtain the single room which became our home for the next four years. This was the home to which I returned from the childrens' camp in Saxony.

"In many ways we were better off than others. When the bombing raids began, my parents had each taken into the shelter two canvas bags. These bags taken by my father contained stock: spectacle frames and lenses, as well as hand tools and instruments from his shop; those taken by my mother had money and anything of value from our home that she could fit into the bag. She had also carried blankets and had worn her fur coat.

"So although my father had to be bullied, goaded, cajoled and helped by my mother to even begin turning a partially destroyed building into a shop, he actually had at hand the means to make a new start.

"During that first winter in our one-room home, we were often without heating. The three of us huddled together in one bed wearing as many clothes as we had to put on. My father often wore his overcoat, hat, mittens, even balaclava, in his shop.

"My father and I each developed a cough. My mother pronounced the need for more varied food than daily bread and twice-a-week pickled cucumber. With her new-found tenacity, my mother went from end to end of our village, then beyond, until she uncovered what she had interrogated and interrogated to discover.

"In spite of severe penalties for doing so, there must have been many farmers selling food on the black market. Those of whom my mother came to learn, were some hundred-and-twenty kilometers away. She also learned they would not take money. Little status was given to money because of the paucity of goods to buy, and also the widespread belief that money would become devalued and devalued again, as it had following World War I.

"My mother began leaving home when it was still dark, before morning and arriving home long after evening darkness had fallen. In between, she traveled a hundred-and-fifteen kilometers by train, then five kilometers by foot. She was, she told us, rarely more than ten minutes at the farm, before she began her journey home.

"This journey was undertaken twice each week. I began to notice rings missing from my mother's fingers, the chiming clock went from the mantlepiece and was replaced by my father's fob watch. Photographs of both my parents' parents now stood without their gold frames and plates of Dresden china and vases of Venetian glass were seen no more.

"In return, we at times had cheese. Sometimes there was milk (brought all that distance in a saucepan with a lid), sometimes cream, or a chicken, or eggs; twice or three times there was pork.

"Once my mother took me with her. I remember the station platform covered by a dirty sludge of snow and inside the carriage there was also snow because the train windows had been shattered during bombing raids. I carried a pair of boots I had long since outgrown and a gold filigree frame that the day before had contained my parents' wedding photograph and another gold filigree frame that previously had shown my father in his burgomaster's regalia.

"My mother was, in a sense, wearing her Frau Burgomaster regalia: her fur coat. My father bought it for her when he became burgomaster. The fur coat expressed his belief that a burgomaster's wife should have such a coat. As such, the coat was more a symbol of his once-held pride than her's. Normally, my mother did not value such things so highly; yet she counted her fur coat her greatest possession. This was less due to ownership of the coat itself, than knowing my father had to borrow money to buy it and had taken years paying back the loan and interest.

"At this early hour, the lights of station platforms, street lamps and house lights slid backwards past the train. Then came the morning, as gray as roofing slates, through which fields and rivers, towns and villages slid past. We came among hills, and my mother said, 'Now we are in Bavaria.'

"Later, we were walking and it began to rain. We continued on our way in the rain along a road that climbed between agricultural land without crop or animal to a cluster of houses around a church with onion-shaped spires crowning the hilltop. From one hilltop village we descended past frozen agricultural land to forest in a valley, up out of forest through frozen agricultural land to another hilltop village.

"Here my mother went up steps to rap at a door. Her knocking was answered by a wide-hipped, wide-bosomed, wide-shouldered woman who constantly wiped her hands on her apron. The wide woman did not greet or speak to my mother. She walked past us, down steps to beneath the house. She drew back a sliding door that was as wide as four normal doors.

"We all stepped inside, into an odor pungent with manure and urine and milk and straw. The wide woman called. She did not wait for an answer or acknowledgment to her call. She stepped out from the barn, closing shut the sliding door.

9

"Enclosed within the pungent odor, I saw cows in stalls all the way along one wall and halfway along the wall opposite. Platforms above the stalls held straw and cattlebeet. There were hens all over the straw and in the stalls unoccupied by cows.

"One stall, not occupied by a cow, contained two high piles of carpets. Another had high piles of clothes, mostly overcoats. Many stalls had wooden boxes with the lids open. It was impossible to close the lids on the mirrors, vases, crockery, picture frames, paintings, books, shoes and boots that rose high out of each box.

"Hens had left their droppings on piled coats and the jumble of mirrors, boots, books. There was cow shit over coats and carpets.

"A man came towards us. At my mother's prompting, I showed him the boots. My mother asked for cheese.

"'Not worth cheese,' the man said. 'I'll give you milk.'

"He tossed my boots on the jumble spilling out of one box, and went to the far end of the barn. Returning, he handed me our saucepan. By the weight I could tell it was no more than half full of milk.

"I gave the farmer the gold filigree frames, and received one egg for each.

"Then my mother took off her fur coat. She got six eggs for that.

"The farmer tossed the fur coat on top of carpets that had cow dung on them. I thought my mother was going to cry.

"She didn't. She turned from the farmer, wrenched back the sliding door, strode from the barn out onto the road. She walked fast, so very fast I had to run to keep up. I complained of her pace. She handed me a single slice of rye bread she had brought with her, and kept walking just as fast. She kept up that pace walking downhill past frozen agricultural land toward forest, uphill out of forest through frozen agricultural land toward a hilltop village with its onion-spired church, downhill through agricultural land again—all the way to the railway station.

"That night my father had news. An American soldier had come into his shop wanting a new side on his reading spectacles and a new lens for his sunglasses. When the American returned, he pronounced himself well satisfied. He tossed a high denomination

D-mark note onto the shop counter.

"My father had difficulty finding sufficient change. While he searched his money drawer, the American took from his pocket a chocolate bar and peeled back the wrapping. As my father counted out the change, the American bit into the chocolate bar. My father looked up from counting—to stare at the chocolate bar. He couldn't help himself (he told us) because he was constantly hungry, and because it was years since he had seen such a chocolate bar, and most of all because he was appalled at the American's manners.

"The American laughed. He scooped up his change, thrust the chocolate bar into my father's hand, and left.

"My father showed my mother and me the chocolate bar which still had teeth marks where one end was bitten off.

"Perhaps the gesture of giving the chocolate bar to my father had been intended to be kindly, but my father only saw in it the arrogance of a conqueror toward one who has been conquered.

"He was even more appalled that he—once proprietor of a very fine shop, member of a profession that once counted Spinoza as a member, once burgomaster, once respected committee-man—should have fallen so low as to actually accept the part-eaten chocolate bar.

"My mother said nothing. Not then. She took a knife and cut close to the teeth marks, With two further cuts she divided the remainder into three equal pieces.

"Taking the piece I was offered, I chewed very slowly so I could make it last, trying to hold it in my mouth without quite swallowing all of that sticky creamy sweetness.

"My father did not take the piece my mother pushed toward him. Sitting in his chair, he leaned forward to cover his face with his hands.

"Now my mother did speak. She ordered me to bed. I was underneath the blankets when I realized my mother could not have previously told my father she was going to exchange her fur coat for eggs, because she was telling him now. As she told him, she chewed and chewed on her piece of the chocolate bar and kept pushing toward my father the plate with his piece still on it.

"I saw my father's head sink lower and lower until it was right against his knees.

"Lying there, I ran the tip of my tongue along the back of my teeth to capture the last bit of sweetness. And as I drifted off to sleep, I wondered if my mother could possibly have made that first cut even closer to the teeth marks...

"In the morning, the plate was still on the table. The last piece of chocolate bar was gone."

In the airport restaurant, only the three of us remained at a table. The waitress was changing tablecloths while pointedly looking in our direction.

Arthur indicated the almost empty restaurant; he was the other Australian.

"A lot of us," Arthur said, "have had to swallow—I mean really swallow—our pride."

Hans picked up the bill, took it to the waitress and handed her the bill and his credit card.

Walking from the restaurant, Arthur and I took out our wallets and began counting out our shares. Hans waved our wallets back into our pockets. We comfortably accepted his courtesy, knowing he heads a leading firm in his industry.

Hans continued: "It was more than his pride that my father swallowed. He had to gulp down his previous attitudes to the way things had been. Yet, it was also the prelude to his resurrection as a person. Or rather, the prelude to a new beginning for both my father and mother. Soon after that, my mother came into his business—no longer as an appendage to him—as an equal partner. Within three years, they'd left that shop. They started manufacturing optical tools and instruments, subcontracting to others work they were unable to do themselves. They arranged distribution throughout Germany, both of what they manufactured and what they had made for them by others. After I completed my formal education, I joined my parents' business and extended distribution into export. It's come a long way since then; but I never forget it was my parents, together, who laid the foundation of the business."

Hans, Arthur and I went to make our phone calls to reschedule our business appointments. Arthur and I looked at each other and recognized that we both respected Hans for his deep regard for his parents but even more for his honesty in giving so much credit to both his mother and father for the success of their worldwide business. Human nature being what it is, I wondered how many other heads of large, successful firms would be so forthright in giving credit to the firm's founders...especially if they were one's parents.

Graham Sheil, a compulsive writer whose short stories are published "by just about everyone in Australia who publishes short stories," worked his way from laborer and pick-'n'-shovel miner to proprietorship of an optical wholesale company. But the need to write has never waned. His work appears in magazines, newspapers, anthologies and his own collection of short stories. This story won the Symes Newspaper Award for Short Stories in 1985. Mr. Sheil now also writes plays and novels.

"The thought of their faces when they saw
the empty platter almost convulsed him..."

The Vagabond

BY MARY DRAKE

IN spite of the slight pain in his leg, in spite of the horrible thing
that had just happened, he whistled as he limped along the dusty
road.

The morning had started off with no special promise, but now,
before the sun had reached its zenith, his fortunes had changed.
He grinned to himself as he shifted his rolled-up coat to the other
arm. Knowing what it contained, its weight was a pleasure.

But he didn't want to think about the last half hour. He didn't
want to think about the woman, or the cut on his leg and all that
blood. He hated violence, and avoided it whenever possible. Come
to think of it, it was the first time he'd ever used violence, if you
didn't count that dog he'd had to kill in a barn one night.

He was a vagabond. It was a life that suited him well: traveling
on foot, living one day to the next, not knowing what each one
would bring. Sometimes he'd stop at a gas station and ask if he
could use the phone. He'd go into the office and riffle through the

telephone book, waiting till a car pulled up for gas. Then when the attendant was busy he'd quickly open the desk drawer. Quite often there was money in it. He wouldn't take much, just a couple of bucks that wouldn't be missed, and then he'd leave twenty cents on the desk for the phone call he'd never made.

He'd thank the guy on his way out, and stop and yarn for a minute to allay suspicion. It was surprising how often that little plan had worked for him. A nice small profit and a quick getaway with no one hurt, that was his line. It was the key to his success, really—never be greedy for the big stuff. Just take a little at a time, enough for his creature comforts.

He wasn't above doing a bit of work occasionally. At the farmhouses along the country roads you could generally count on a good square meal in return for mowing a lawn, mending a broken fence, or painting a barn. It helped to keep him in good nick. And ten to one, while he ate in the kitchen, there'd be an opportunity for a quick look round for money. It was quite pathetic the way these country women always chose the same places for their small hoard of ready cash. If there was a shelf above the stove you could almost count on finding something stashed away in an old teapot or sugar bowl...

What had just happened in that old house wasn't in his line at all, but things had got out of hand. He was anxious to get away from it as soon as possible, and looked behind him, ready to thumb a ride from the first passing vehicle.

He didn't have long to wait. A large truck gave noisy warning of its approach, and the driver slowed down at his signal. He climbed into the cabin with a muttered word of thanks.

"Going far?" the driver asked conversationally.

"Just as far as you can take me, mate," he answered. He had to almost shout above the roar of the engine and the noise of the *tranny* that was blaring out pop music from somewhere at his feet.

He was conscious of the *truckie*'s curious scrutiny. On this road there was a mighty long stretch between one town and the next, and only a few isolated houses between. He knew he didn't look like a tramp. He was clean-shaven and neatly dressed, and carried no gear except for what was in his rolled-up coat. He was ready with a glib explanation.

"I'm a doctor," he said briefly. "Had a slight coronary not long ago, and prescribed a walking tour for myself. Best cure there is—no phone or patients to worry you, and plenty of exercise. A good way to see the country too. I thumb a ride now and then, and generally put up at some cheap pub for the night."

He liked the story he made up on the spur of the moment, about being a doctor. He'd never told that one before, but it had come readily to his lips. He prided on never telling the same story twice. "Should have been a ruddy writer," he told himself. "With my imagination."

"You sure travel light," the *truckie* was saying with a glance at the rolled-up coat he was carrying.

He grinned. "A razor and a change of underwear in a plastic bag. A few bucks and a checkbook in my pocket. What more do I need?"

After that they didn't talk, and he was glad of it. He closed his eyes, feigning sleep. The episode at that last house had shaken him up more than he cared to admit. He didn't want to think about what had happened, but in spite of himself, as the truck rattled along the unsealed road, vivid pictures of the last half-hour flashed behind his closed eyes.

He'd been walking along at a leisurely pace, scuffing his feet among the leaves and debris on the dusty road. It was a brisk invigorating morning. White clouds scudded across the blue sky, and a boisterous wind whistled through the trees.

Round a bend he had suddenly come to an old dilapidated house, set back from the road. It was like a child's drawing—a door in the middle flanked on either side by a window, with two dormer windows above. He hesitated at the gate, his hand on the latch. It had been a long walk since the last township, and he could do with a cup of tea and something to eat. The morning was so pleasant that he'd even consider doing a job of work for a meal.

He'd opened the gate and walked up to the front door. There was no response to his knock so he'd gone round to the back. A woman—an enormous woman, not young—was hanging clothes on the line. Her back was turned to him, and her ample body bulged above and below the strings of her apron. Her sleeves were rolled up above the elbows, revealing large fleshy arms, and her abundant graying hair was drawn up into a huge bun. She was trying to peg a large sheet to the line, fighting against the gusty wind.

He was about to speak when he noticed the open kitchen door, only a few feet away. Her back was still turned to him and without hesitating, he slipped inside. On quick light footsteps he passed through the kitchen and mounted the stairs.

The first room he came to was a bedroom. From the window he could see the woman bending over a basket, her mouth full of pegs. He quickly searched the wardrobe and dressing table and then looked under the bed. He saw a battered old bag of gray vinyl, its zipper broken. He pulled it out and his heart leapt when he opened it. Neat bundles of notes, each secured with a rubber band. He slipped one roll into his trouser pocket for immediate use, shrugged out of his jacket and rolled up the bag inside it.

A sudden movement at the door caused him to turn. The woman was standing there. She didn't look afraid, she looked murderous. She'd struggled like a wild thing when he went for her, and no wonder, when she was fighting for that dough. Probably her life savings. He wouldn't have believed there was so much strength in those fat arms.

She'd broken loose for a moment, and picking up a heavy glass vase from the bedside table, had thrown it at him with all her strength. If it had hit him it would have been curtains, but it struck the opposite wall with a terrific crash and shattered into a thousand pieces. Glass flew everywhere, and he was aware of a sharp stinging pain in his leg, just above the ankle.

Then she came at him like a tigress, her black eyes blazing in her round face. Her enormous bulk seemed to envelop his thin frame. He realized he was fighting for his life, and when his thin fingers found her neck they dug deep into the soft folds of fat. Deeper and deeper, till she was still, and the struggle was over.

He hadn't panicked. He'd gone into the bathroom and washed

his hands, then he'd left the woman where she lay and gone downstairs. He became conscious of the cut on his leg. It was bleeding profusely, and a red trail marked his passage across the kitchen floor.

He'd sat down at the table to examine his injury. There was a sliver of glass embedded in the flesh, sharp and fine as an icicle. Gritting his teeth, he grasped it between thumb and finger and pulled it out. The flow of blood immediately increased, and dragging up his grimy black sock he'd pressed it hard against the wound till the bleeding eased a little. The sight of so much blood unnerved him, but it didn't hurt much, and he was anxious to get away from the place.

He'd limped out to the backyard, and noticed an old bicycle leaning against the wall. For a moment he considered taking it, but then decided it was too risky. Someone might recognize it, and besides, he would get away from the area much quicker by thumbing a ride. Then the first thing he'd do when he came to a town was take a room at a pub, and count the stuff. He could picture the notes spread all over the bed, and the thought excited him. He'd never had so much money at the one time. But first he'd have to do something about his leg and the blood.

He looked at the line of washing dancing crazily to the rhythm of the wind. A sheet had twisted itself round the line and got caught in a rose bush that climbed the post. There were two small jagged rents in it from the thorns. It was a check flannelette sheet, thin and faded from much use, and tore easily in his hands from where the thorns had pierced the fabric. He folded the long triangular strip and wound it tightly round the cut. Instantly it felt better. He pulled up his sock and hardly limped at all when he left the place. It wasn't till he'd gone a couple of miles that it began to throb, and he'd sure been glad to see this truck...

He shook his head a little, as though to clear it from his thoughts, and opened his eyes. The truckie glanced at him sideways.

"You O.K., mate? You look a bit white about the gills."

"Yes, yes. I'm fine," he said hastily. The last thing he wanted was to rouse this guy's suspicions. He touched his chest. "I've walked too far this morning, I guess. The old ticker gets a bit tired."

"Maybe you should get off at the next town and rest up awhile," the truckie suggested.

"Yes, I think I'll do that," he agreed tiredly.

"Been on the road for some time?"

"Nearly a month now. Time I went home. Time I saw the wife and kids again."

"Where's home?"

"Sydney."

"Jeez, you've come a long way."

"It won't take me long to get back. I'll catch a train, or maybe hop a plane. How long before we hit the next town?"

"About half-an-hour. I'd put up at the Sunshine Motel, if I were you. You can get a good breakfast in your room, and there's all mod cons—telly, fridge, toaster and jug, the lot. Nothing classy, mind you, but it's cheap and clean."

"Thanks," he said wearily. "I'll do that."

Suddenly he felt tired, drained. Maybe it was all that blood he'd lost.

When he said good-bye to the truckie he put his hand tentatively in his pocket. The man saw the gesture.

"No charge, mate," he said with a friendly grin. "I was glad of the company."

Before going to the motel he bought a suitcase. Nothing fancy, but not a cheap one either. Just a good solid-looking case, in which he put the old gray vinyl bag and his jacket. He didn't want to arrive without any luggage.

He checked in at the Sunshine Motel and once in his room, locked the door. There were no frills, no wall-to-wall carpet or anything like that, but as the truckie had said, it had all mod cons. His hands were shaking as he took out the vinyl bag and spilled its contents onto the bed.

The bundles of notes were made up into totals of twenty dollar bills. Good, he thought. No large notes to cash. He counted them. Two hundred—two hundred and fifty—three hundred. Altogether there were three hundred and twenty dollars. Not bad. Not bad at all.

He felt on top of the world. Or would have, if it hadn't been for the bloody throbbing pain in his leg. Suddenly he felt so tired that he thought it maybe wouldn't be a bad idea to shack up here for a few days. He could afford it now—no problem there—and he could watch telly and just relax till his leg healed. He'd stock up with food and grog, and maybe some newspapers and magazines. That way he could have a real rest, not even have to leave his room for meals. He'd tell them at the desk that he didn't want to be disturbed. He could say he was a writer, or something like that, and had a lot of work to do...

It was getting dark when he went out for provisions. The main shops had closed, but he was able to buy all that he needed in a small store, and then stopped at a pub for a bottle of whisky. The lighted windows of the large shops were gaily decorated, and he realized it would soon be Christmas. Well, one day was the same as another to him. He couldn't remember celebrating Christmas since he was a kid, except for that "celebration" (if you could call it that) a few years ago. He grinned at the memory.

He felt too tired to eat when he got back to his motel room, but he had a couple of drinks and then fell into a heavy sleep. When he woke in the early hours of the morning he had a raging thirst. There was no air-conditioning, and though he had left his window wide open, his body felt on fire. The heat seemed to spread right through his whole body, though it was worse in his sore leg. He switched on the light to see if the bleeding had stopped. He'd left the bandage on with the sock over it when he got into bed.

He was relieved to see there was only a slight stain on the outside of the bandage. He was tempted to take it off to examine the wound, but decided to leave it alone in case the bleeding started again.

He fell into a fitful sleep, and much later, when the girl knocked on the door to do his room, he told her to leave it. As the day wore on he kept promising himself to get up and make a cup of coffee or something, but didn't. It would have been good, he thought wistfully, to have someone to look after him, to sponge him with cold water, and put ice-packs on his wound. He wondered uneasily if he'd got an infection in it, remembering how he'd tried to stop the bleeding with his grimy sock.

The only times he left his bed were to go to the bathroom, and each time he drank copious quantities of water. He had a thirst he couldn't quench, and his body felt on fire.

He began to lose track of time. The fever made him dream a lot, mostly nightmares. Once he thought he heard the pealing of bells, and wondered if it was Christmas Day. It brought to mind that "celebration" a few years ago, and he began to think about it, to distract his mind from the throbbing and the pain...

He'd been walking through a small country town at dusk on Christmas night, feeling just a bit low and depressed because through the cottage windows he caught frequent glimpses of decorated trees. There was the sound of children's laughter and appetizing smells of roast turkey and mince pies. He'd felt his mouth watering. There was an unaccustomed longing inside him, not just for the festive food, but a longing to be part of a family, sharing a Christmas meal. Something that was just a vague childhood memory.

He'd walked through the length of the small town, until he came to the last house. Beyond that there was only a church and an old cemetery. The house was a comfortable stone one on a corner block. Through the front window he'd seen a gray-haired man sitting at a piano, playing carols. A group of children stood around him, singing.

"Peace on earth..." The high childish trebles had drifted out on the still air, and there was a lump in his throat.

Bloody sentimental fool! he'd thought angrily. He decided to go round to the back door. Surely he wouldn't be refused a bite to eat on such a night, in this season of goodwill?

He passed the front window with its sweet sounds of carols, and went around the corner, keeping outside the low stone wall. The dining room was on this side. Through the lighted window he could see the festive table with its shining cutlery and its bowls of raisins and nuts. There were streamers, and a bunch of balloons hung from the overhead light.

A woman bustled into the room, carrying a large platter. She wore an apron over her fine dress, and in the strong light he could see perspiration beading her face from the heat of the kitchen.

There was a brown, succulent-looking turkey on the platter, and she placed it at the head of the table which was near the open window. His nose twitched as he caught the tantalizing odor of the bird.

The woman untied her apron strings and went through to the front room. In a minute the sound of carols ceased, and he guessed she'd called them to the table.

He'd acted then, almost without thinking. With one leap he was over the stone wall, and a moment later he had climbed through the open window and grabbed the hot turkey in his hands.

As he'd raced towards the corner, a backward look showed him that the front room was already empty. It had been a near thing. The thought of their faces when they saw the empty platter almost convulsed him, and he laughed so much that he could hardly run. But he knew he had to make a quick getaway. They'd be after him in full cry when they found their Christmas dinner had been snatched from under their noses.

The shadow of the old church had loomed up in front of him, and beyond that the cemetery. Better to hide, he'd thought, than try to outrun them. He hadn't noticed the heat of the bird when he first grabbed it, but with each step he took it seemed to become hotter. It was burning his fingers and he tossed it from one hand to the other as he ran, laughing fit to burst.

It was not yet late, but to his relief some storm clouds had gathered, bringing early darkness. The old cemetery was full of shadows as he'd made his way to the farthest corner.

He'd sat on a gravestone, leaned comfortably back and had begun the feast. It was the best meal he'd ever eaten. He'd had nothing all day, and very little the day before. His eager hands tore the bird apart and he gorged himself, the rich juices running between his fingers and down his chin. A couple of times he thought he heard voices, but he was safe in his hidden corner.

The storm clouds rolled away. A sickle moon rode the sky and the stars winked down on him as though they were sharing the joke. Crazy! Crazy!

He'd eaten till he could eat no more. If only he'd had a newspaper he could have wrapped what was left of the bird. Well, the local dogs and cats could have a treat this Christmas night. He'd tossed the remains among the tombstones, on to the already well-fertilized hallowed ground. Then he'd taken to the road, laughing so much that anyone would have thought he was tipsy...

He'd often chuckled when he thought about that night, but now the memory brought only a weak smile. A tear of self-pity coursed down his cheek. He slept...

Once he heard (or dreamed he heard) someone knocking at his door. And later he had a confused impression of being lifted from his bed and moved somewhere else. There were strange voices, strange sounds, strange hands ministering to him, and a strong smell of antiseptic. He guessed vaguely that he was in a hospital, but felt too ill to care...

There came a morning when he felt better. A lot better. His body felt cool and light and comfortable, and his stomach told him he was hungry. But though the fever had gone, the nightmares hadn't. For the worst nightmare was about to begin.

The door opened, and a man in a white coat who looked like a doctor came in.

"You've been ill," he said, sitting down by the bed. "An infected leg. Septicaemia." His voice was cold, dispassionate. "But you're over the worst now. Well enough to see visitors."

"Visitors?" he asked weakly. That was a laugh, that was. Did this guy think there was going to be a string of friends and relations coming in? Bringing him flowers, holding his hand?

"Yes," the cold voice continued. "Two visitors have been waiting to see you for some days, but you haven't been well enough. Not till today."

"Two visitor?" he asked warily. "Who are they?"

"The police. They want to question you about the murder of a woman. She lived some distance from here, and was well-known in her district. She used to ride a bicycle, carrying a gray vinyl bag wherever she went. The bag was found in your motel room."

He closed his eyes for a moment, and when he opened them again the doctor's face was swimming crazily—far away one minute, then coming close, looming right up in front of him.

"And," that cold voice continued, "the strip of bandage that we removed from your leg matched a torn sheet that was hanging on her clothesline. The bloodstains on her kitchen floor matched your shoe. I think you're well enough now to see your visitors. I'll show them in."

A lively, handsome woman, Mary Drake has been writing for 20 years and has had more than 200 stories published, mostly in Australia, but also in England and the Scandinavian countries. "The Vagabond" won first prize in the North Shore Times Competition in Sydney. She has written a great deal of poetry which has been read over the Australian Broadcasting Commission; she has also written several plays which have been produced. The first $1,000 earned by her writings was donated to the Australian Society of Authors which set up a biannual short story competition called the Mary Drake Award. Mary Drake is the creator of a lovely American Beauty shade of hibiscus called by her name.

"He had stayed here all alone and worked hard,
but what for?"

Spring Festival Eve

BY DA LI

THE last customer came in at 6:30, to buy vinegar rather than to
eat. She was all dressed up and her plump cheeks were red with
cold. Out of breath, she was clutching a bottle in her chubby little
hand.

"Mister," she begged, "can I buy some vinegar?" She looked up
and handed a bottle to Cui Ming. "Mummy wants to make sweet-
and-sour fish, but my brother spilled the vinegar."

Cui Ming went to the kitchen and poured some vinegar into the
bottle. As a rule, privately run restaurants weren't supposed to sell
provisions, but this was Spring Festival Eve and if someone
urgently needed some vinegar, you really couldn't say no. If the
town authorities got to hear about it and ticked him off, he would
just have to pay the penalty.

The little girl took the vinegar, thanked him and rushed out.

Cui Ming picked up the money she left and spread it out on the
counter. It was fifty fen! He quickly ran out, but the girl was long

gone. A bottle of vinegar was only ten fen and she would get told off by her parents. Perhaps someone from her family would come to ask for the change. If they didn't, he'd find her and return it. His place wasn't open on Spring Festival Eve to earn forty fen that way; he'd earn four or even forty yuan honestly! He and Jin Xiaocui, the waitress, had had a heated argument about money earlier that evening.

"I've already said a hundred times, who'd give up a big family dinner on Spring Festival Eve and come here to eat?"

"Don't be so sure about that. Fingers are all different lengths—who knows?"

"Even if you get a few customers, how much can you make?" Xiaocui said, finishing her washing up.

"The more the better. If it's only a little, well that's that."

"You really are pigheaded!" Xiaocui said, buttoning up her dark green parka. Scowling, she thrust her hands into the pockets. "Let's close up and you come and have dinner with us."

"No," Cui Ming muttered, rubbing his hands with a towel.

"You..." Xiaocui hesitated for a moment. "If you don't come, my father'll be furious."

Xiaocui's father, Jin, was the chef. To get the family dinner ready in time, he'd stoked up the stove that afternoon and left the cleaning up to the two younger people.

A few days back, he'd said to Cui Ming, "Since you're not going back to Beijing, I hope you'll come and spend the evening at our place, so that we'll have some company."

But each time Cui Ming just smiled and didn't reply.

"Let's go!" Xiaocui urged. "My father'll be getting impatient."

"No," Cui Ming said, carefully wiping a table. "Go home and give him a hand with the cooking. Let me stay here to wait on a few more customers tonight."

"All you can think of is making money." Xiaocui angrily flung a pale blue scarf round her neck.

"What's wrong with that? It's all my own work."

"But all you care about is money." Xiaocui wrapped her scarf round again, marched out and slammed the door.

Night fell and the street lights went on.

Cui Ming walked outside and turned on the restaurant sign lights. Immediately the name *Guest Welcome Cafe* stood out on the signboard. His gloom and anxiety left him.

Xiaocui's anger hadn't weakened his determination. He felt absolutely certain it would be a good night for business. They were located just in front of the railway station and near the busy center of the seaside town. Usually there were plenty of seafood places open to attract customers and they didn't have a chance to shine. Tonight the others were all closed, and their small cafe could take advantage of that. He didn't believe that there wouldn't be a soul on the streets tonight. Later on in the evening, six passenger trains would arrive and hungry travelers would probably come in for a bite, because only his place was open.

In the hour since Xiaocui's departure however, only the little girl had come in.

He suddenly felt hungry. Despite all the poultry, meat and seafood piled up on the chopping board, he was in no mood for cooking. It was over half a year since he'd learned from Jin how to boil, bake, fry and roast; he could even prepare a banquet by himself. But now he just didn't feel like doing it. His skill was in serving customers and in making money. If he cooked such delicacies for himself, he would be losing money.

Finally he ate a bowl of plain noodles cooked in a small quantity of soup. It was only when his forehead started perspiring that he realized the room was too hot. The ventilator in the backyard was whirring and would probably do so the whole night.

That afternoon Aung Geng from the building neighborhood committee had come to collect money, saying that each family had to donate at least fifty fen to reward old Chai for putting in overtime to keep the boiler going. He'd given up Spring Festival dinner with his family and instead would be bustling in and out of the smoky boiler room all night long, so he deserved some thanks. At around four, Cui had seen the slightly stooped Chai grinning from ear to ear. That was when Aunt Geng had given him a wad of money. Over fourteen yuan, from twenty-eight families, plus double-time that day amounted to more than twenty yuan.

"Can't I equal that?" The buzzing ventilator annoyed him and he opened a window to let in some air. Through the window he could see a luminous orange hand on the railway station clock pointing at 8. The express train from Harbin was due ten minutes ago, why weren't there lots of passengers streaming out? Then he remembered there wouldn't be many travelers on Spring Festival night. Hadn't he always left for home a week or so earlier when he was in the countryside?

There wasn't a soul on the quiet street. Usually there was a constant din of tram bells, but tonight you could scarcely hear a thing.

Cui Ming liked the sound of the tram bells. He was used to it. He remembered how nice it had been as a child to nestle up to his mother and listen to the pelting rain and the lilting bells before falling asleep. Now and again blue sparks from the tram wires flickered across his dreams. He'd often dreamed that he was in a white captain's uniform standing on the bridge of an ocean liner. On the quay in the bright sunshine, his mother and sister would be waving scarves welcoming him home.

He had dreamed a lot of beautiful dreams in that room overlooking the street. But now it had become the *Guests Welcome Cafe* and he was left to spend Spring Festival evening alone in his empty nest.

He couldn't stop himself from reaching into his pocket again. His mother had sent him a telegram three days earlier telling him to come home. His father was a surgeon in Beijing and his mother had been transferred there last spring. He had a sister at middle school too. But he couldn't go. He was studying at the television university and if he'd gone with them, he would have had to pull out of school and give up his job. He'd been a waiter at the machine tool factory canteen where his mother worked. His mother hated to leave her son there alone, but he didn't want to abandon his schooling and his four years in the job. Worst of all, he had hated the thought of parting with his girl friend Bai Lin.

He'd got to know Bai Lin when they were both doing manual labor in the countryside and the two of them had been together for eight years. At that time her father, a bureau chief, had been sent to a mountain village to do manual labor too. Cui Ming had acted as her bodyguard and Bai Lin, like an orphaned kitten, had become very attached to him.

After returning to the city, Bai Lin had become a bus conductor and was then transferred to do office work in the trade union of the bus company. She hadn't forgotten him but she didn't much like his working as a waiter.

"Sit another university entrance examination this year," she'd said softly, nestled against his chest, her imploring eyes on his face. "This time you can apply for the school of arts and sciences."

Cui Ming stroked her long sleek hair and silently gave her forehead a gentle kiss. He was lacking in confidence because he had already failed twice. When they'd been in that mountain village a hundred li from the county seat, she hadn't objected to his ploughing the fields. So why did she push him to sit the college entrance examination now?

Finally he passed the entrance exam for the television university. Actually he'd only done it for her. And if he left, it would mean losing her. That was no good! Bai Lin already belonged to him. She had been his since that summer when the two of them had stayed the night in a shed near the maize field. But how could he tell his mother all this?

When his mother had wanted to take him away, he had summoned up all of his courage to protest, "You and Dad have lived apart more than twenty years. Do you really want to make me and Bai Lin do the same thing?"

His mother gave in. Her son had grown up and wanted to fend for himself. As a mother she had to acknowledge that.

His mother and sister went back to Beijing, leaving him in this large, deserted house. He'd spent so many unforgettable days here, especially at Spring Festival when his father had come for a fortnight. The whole place would ring with laughter. Festival eve was the high point. Everyone dressed his best. His parents sat by the radio making dumplings, while he and his sister set off fireworks outside. But tonight he was all alone with nobody to talk to. He regretted he hadn't listened to his mother and gone back to Beijing for the holiday.

He felt lonely. Central TV had special programs so he switched

29

on the set, only to find a lot of interference on the screen caused by the backyard blower. Suddenly, the picture cleared and a female singer appeared. The blower must have been switched off. He looked at his watch, it wasn't yet ten.

"The old fox, he's got his money, but he won't put in any more work. It's still too early to knock off," he said out loud. Suddenly the door creaked open and in came a small, thin, hunchbacked old man. It was old Chai.

"So you've finished, Chai?" Cui Ming greeted him enthusiastically, a habit he'd acquired serving customers the last few months, whatever his real mood was.

"No, not yet," the old man said, pulling a towel from round his neck to wipe the soot from his face. "The water's much too hot already. I've banked the fire for a bit so there's no work for me at the moment."

Cui Ming pulled out a folding chair and gave it a wipe with his cloth. "Take a breather, Chai. You've got the building pretty hot tonight. Look, I opened the window."

"Not only you. Almost everyone else's windows are open too." He was obviously pleased with himself. "That's why I came here, to have a drink."

"Then it's just the right time for some good wine from the Feng-cheng Cellars." Cui Ming took a square bottle from a shelf behind the counter. It was wrapped in cellophane and had a red ribbon around its neck. Cui Ming pointed at the label on the bottle: "See the English words, it's for export."

Chai picked it up and gave it a close look. "Great, it's from my home." He immediately perked up. "No wonder I haven't seen this for so long, it's being exported. How much is a bottle?"

"I got it wholesale, four yuan twenty." Actually he'd bought it for three yuan eighty through someone he knew. But one day he'd have to pay back the favor and where would that money come from?

"Gracious, it used to sell for less than two yuan."

"But didn't you know, a yuan today is worth only forty-six per cent of its past value."

"Yes, prices are going up," he sighed. "Pour two ounces for me, will you?"

"Sure." Cui Ming placed a glass, a plate and some chopsticks in front of him.

Chai pushed the chopsticks aside. "I only want a drink, not anything to eat."

"It's a shame not to have something to eat with good wine like that." Cui Ming put the chopsticks back. "Why don't I give you some cold cuts as an appetizer and after that you can have some sauté shrimp?"

"No." Chai waved his hand. "Just some peanuts will do fine."

"Look at you," Cui Ming wouldn't give up, "it's Spring Festival Eve. Why are you holding yourself back? Honestly, everybody's having something wonderful tonight. And you can afford it. How can you be so hard on yourself at your age?"

Chai smiled. "You won't let me go tonight until I've put my hand in my pocket, will you?" Well, give me a cold plate then."

Cui Ming immediately put a large dish on the table. It was shaped like a plum flower and made of cold chicken, clams, smoked fish, preserved eggs, green peas and jellyfish.

"How much is this?" Chai asked, picking up his chopsticks.

"What's the hurry? Eat first and then we can settle up." Cui Ming poured him a glass of wine.

Chai just smiled. "Well, you don't have to get too anxious since you know I've got plenty of money in my pocket tonight. Fifty fen of yours too, you young rascal. I see you've made up your mind to get it back."

"You misunderstood." Cui Ming remained unruffled. "You didn't spend your holiday at home, and instead put in overtime to get the boiler going for all of us; you deserve the extra money."

"That's not it," retorted Chai, chewing on a chicken wing. "I wasn't after money. Tonight's Little Yan's shift, but he wanted to change with me so he could go to his girl friend's. I wasn't that keen. I'm getting on and my Spring Festivals are getting fewer and fewer. My daughter and son have both come from other provinces and we all wanted to have a family reunion dinner. But then I thought, well it's not easy for a young boilerman to find a girl friend, so I gave in. I can manage. Anyway, the boiler can't go off at Spring Festival. Doesn't everyone want their heating tonight?"

"Well it seems you're a pretty noble person! All the more reason to reward yourself with good food I think. How about some fish?"

"No, no thanks!" countered Chai, putting his hand over his pocket as though the money might fly out. "I've got to keep some for my grandchildren tomorrow morning."

On television an actor was miming someone having a hard time eating very tough chicken. Cui Ming was beside himself with laughter.

"You can relax. My chicken's very tender; it just slides down your throat."

Chai gave it a poke with his chopsticks. "It's tender enough, but there's not much meat on it."

Cui Ming adjusted the television. "I'm a better judge of how it should be. With wine, you have to nibble at chicken bit by bit. If you want some plumper meat, I'll cook you some diced chicken and capsicum."

The old man pointed his chopsticks at him. "If you're so smart and able to do so much with a chicken, I bet you'll make a fortune one day."

Cui Ming folded his hands in a gesture of thanks. "I'm very grateful for those auspicious words, especially on Spring Festival."

"No need to thank me, I just hope you'll give me more food next time." He wiped his lips and smiled. "By the way, I forgot to ask, how are your mother and sister getting on?"

"They're all right," Cui Ming replied, his eyes glued to the television.

"Why didn't you go back? Your parents must be upset."

"If I'd gone home for the holidays, where could you have got the drink?" He'd intended to poke fun at the old man, but the words had stung him. Why hadn't he gone home? It wasn't hard to imagine his parents and sister in their new flat thinking of him, worrying about him. How happy they would be if he just pushed open the door and appeared in front of them! But what could he take them? And how could he tell them what had happened to him the last few months?

Before the summer vacation, he'd failed four of his final

examinations and hadn't even qualified for the retakes so he'd been struck off the school roll. When Bai Lin heard the news, she'd sat dumbly in a corner for a long time before bursting into tears. She cried as if the news had broken her heart. Cui Ming had gone over and tried to calm her but she suddenly stood up and flounced out the door. She hadn't come to see him since. He'd telephoned several times to arrange to see her, but all he got was a snub, as if she'd never known him.

Tram bells clanged while he tossed and turned in bed. He wondered why Bai Lin was so cruel. They'd been in love for eight years, but it had vanished in an instant. Was that what relationships between people were about? All of the love and promises had been nothing but hypocritical deception.

He'd felt too ashamed to go to the canteen again, so he'd started up the *Guest Welcome Cafe*. Setting it up may have looked easy but in fact he'd gone through a lot of hardships.

The other day, he'd seen Bai Lin walking arm in arm with a young man who had a white university badge pinned to his chest. She'd walked past his place without so much as a glance in his direction. Could she really have forgotten where he lived? It was a place where she'd said so many tender and loving words and where she'd laughed that engaging laugh. But now she cut him dead. He wanted to go and stop her, ask her why she'd ditched him, and then give her a good beating. But he couldn't make himself do it. The moment he closed his eyes he remembered her beautiful eyes, her loving words and her warm breath...

He didn't hate her, he hated himself. He resolved to make his *Guests Welcome Cafe* successful and famous.

Suddenly a truck pulled up outside, and in came three men in dogskin hats and graying sheepskin overcoats.

"Ha, you're still open! You're a good businessman." Leading them was a man with a ruddy face and a booming voice. He turned to the other two: "Shall we warm up here for awhile?"

"Fine." The others were thinner, shorter and older.

Cui Ming guessed they were probably long-distance drivers. "The room's quite warm, why don't you take off your coats or you'll catch cold when you go out later."

Cui Ming helped them hang up their coats and discovered they were wearing brand new uniforms. They had three red stripes round the cuffs, but they didn't look like customs or railway uniforms.

"Where did you come from?" Chai asked.

"From the north end of the street," the red-faced man boomed.

"Where are you going?"

"To the dustbins," he replied, tossing his head back and laughing.

"Oh I see." Chai caught on at last. "The three of you are..." He didn't know what to say.

"We're from the Environmental Protection Bureau," the man said, smoothing down his uniform. "What? Never seen these before, eh? They've just been issued. Today's Spring Festival Eve, so we've got to make a good showing."

"You don't even get time off today?" Cui Ming brought over a pot of tea and three cups.

"Time off?" the red-faced man said. "Why, the dustbins are full to the brims at festivals. How can we take time off?"

"No wonder, everybody's plucking their chickens and ducks," said a man with hair like a hedgehog, holding a cup of tea. "More coal gets burned, so there are more ashes than usual."

"Dammit!" Red Face swore. "Some people always dump their ashes outside the bins and never take that extra step."

"They're not to blame," the third man, who had a beard, pleaded. "The bins were probably overflowing, so they had to."

"Well, it doesn't matter to you," Red Face complained. "You sit up front and don't get wind and ashes in your face. But I've got the job of shoveling up what they leave."

It turned out that the red-faced man was the loader. The bearded fellow and the one with hair like a hedgehog were the truck and the fork-lift drivers. Looking out of the window, Cui Ming saw a yellow truck parked under the street lamp.

"You've worked hard today; we'll treat you to dinner," Whiskers promised.

"Have we got time?" Hedgehog interjected. "We've only made one trip. I'm worried we won't get things finished."

"We've got enough time," Red Face assured them. "Once we've eaten and drunk our fill, we can do twice as much work. Hey, young fellow, what have you got that's good here?"

Cui Ming had been standing next to them waiting for their order. Pouring some more water into the teapot, he smiled broadly. "What would you like to eat? You can have anything you want as long as I can make it."

"What have you got?" Red Face inquired. "You sound as though you've got everything."

"I know we're no match for the big restaurants. But I've kept ready clams, prawns, scallops and sea slugs, as well as poultry, fish and meat."

"You seem to know what you're doing!" Hedgehog licked his lips. "How about making it two yuan per person for the three of us and make it as good as you can."

"Two yuan?" Red Face looked astonished. "What can you get today with two yuan? We've got our double time, night shift subsidy and meal money. What does that come to? This..." He put up five fingers. "If you ask me, we shouldn't begrudge ourselves food tonight. Let's spend what we have. You don't have to treat me, I'll share the cost with you. Who else understands what we put up with? And if we don't look after ourselves, who else will?"

Moved, Hedgehog slapped a five yuan note down on the table. "You're on. It's only once a year, isn't it? I don't give a damn!"

Red Face and Whiskers fished out their five yuan notes.

Cui, managing to contain his delight, gathered up the money and put it by Red Face's hand. "Please keep your money for the moment. If you're satisfied with the meal, we'll settle up afterwards. If not, then it's my treat. But if the three of you want to eat to your hearts' content, you'd better pay extra for drinks."

"Have you got something decent to drink?" the red-faced man asked.

"Ask that old man over there," Cui Ming pointed at Chai. "He's drinking vintage Fengcheng wine. What do you think of it?"

Chai nodded. "It's pretty fine stuff!"

Red Face went over and picked up the glass and sniffed.

"Take a sip!"

He gulped it down and then asked Cui Ming, "Have you got more?"

"Yes, as much as you like. There's still eight ounces left in that bottle. If you want more, I can get you another bottle."

"What do you think, is eight ounces enough?" Red Face asked his mates.

Before they replied Chai interrupted, "Wait a minute, I'd like another measure."

Cui Ming moved into action like a machine. He set out plates and chopsticks, then brought a big cold plate and platter of sliced raw fish placed like a crescent moon decorated with a cabbage heart cut in the shape of a phoenix tail. This was a famous local dish. While they were drinking, bright yellow fried clams were served and these were followed by bright green rape leaves with mushrooms and vermilion prawns. For the final dish, he prepared an assortment of sea slugs, abalone, conch, scallops and shrimps.

Within an hour all six dishes were on the table.

In high spirits, the three men happily proposed a toast to Cui Ming. He sipped a little from a glass, but didn't eat any food.

Seeing them talking and laughing, Chai couldn't help observing, "This young chef really knows a thing or two."

"Hey," Whiskers held up his chopsticks and turned to Chai, "why don't you have a taste? Superb!"

Chai, his back hunched, shuffled over to them and looked at the food. "Marvelous!"

Red Face looked him up and down. "You're still on duty, are you?"

"Yes, I'm working on the boiler for this building."

"You must make a lot of money," Hedgehog put in.

"I do all right!"

"You're too penny-pinching!" Red Face stuffed a sea slug into his mouth. "On Spring Festival Eve all you eat is a cold plate? That won't do your stomach any good."

"Come and join us," Whiskers urged. "We're in the same boat, working shifts at holidays. Come on, share this with us."

"Well, as long as you don't really mind," Chai answered. "I'll share the cost with you."

Before he'd even sat down, Cui Ming had taken his plate over. "Do you want to order something more?"

Chai didn't know what to do.

"Don't put him to any more expense," Red Face declared. "Anyway we can hardly finish eating this and we've got nearly enough to drink."

"I'll pay for the drinks," Chai announced. "The liquor's from my home, that'll be my treat." His hunched back seemed to straighten. He stood up and filled all their glasses. "Drink up. If you want more we can order another bottle. In fact, I earned more than you did tonight. The building collected over ten yuan for me, so you just help yourselves!"

Probably because he was a little tipsy or just in a good mood, he'd revealed his earnings without being asked.

On television a film star was saying how much she missed her parents, especially at the holiday. Then she sang a Sichuan folksong.

"Look," Red Face said with emotion, "she's a big star, but she can't go home for her holidays either. So what have we got to complain about?"

As for Cui Ming, he'd hoped more people would not spend the festival at home and would come to his restaurant instead, so he could make more money. He reckoned the four of them would spend about twenty-one yuan tonight. He'd make over eight yuan, forty per cent profit. Even more, in fact, since the seafood he'd got at a discount from friends. And the other ingredients weren't that expensive either. A lot of his mates who worked at sea stopped by for a drink and Cui would treat them to a meal on the house.

When he started out, people suggested he shouldn't go for too much profit and instead should serve good cheap food in order to get customers and build up his business. This he'd done but he hadn't really made a profit. He thought now it was time to start making a little money.

His four customers were enjoying themselves, but Cui Ming felt tired. He wanted to go to bed, but they kept on with their drinking, and there was still a lot of washing-up waiting to be done. During his twenty-odd years, he'd never been so busy at Spring Festival.

He had stayed here all alone and worked hard, but what for? Only for money? He looked at the four men, they would be going back to work. He could get some sleep later, but they would be busy till dawn. What did they do it for? Only to earn double time? That was not really true but he didn't want to pursue the question further. In any case, he hadn't been wrong to keep his cafe open tonight.

Suddenly he heard the sound of a motorbike outside. Then someone shouted, "Hey Cui, you still open?"

Opening the door, Cui Ming saw it was Jian, the designer from the Rainbow Cinema. He was an art school graduate. Cui's sister had studied painting with him and his whole family respected Jian.

"Why didn't you take the night off?" Cui Ming asked.

"Zhao got ill, so I had to run about carrying films instead." He parked his motorbike and followed Cui Ming inside. When he saw the customers, he gave Cui Ming a knowing smile. "You're a good businessman."

Cui Ming felt embarrassed about talking business with Jian and changed the subject. "Isn't the show finished yet?"

"No, it's still early." Jian pulled off his gloves and warmed his hands on the radiator. "They'll be on all night tonight because there are four films altogether and they only started at ten."

Seeing all-night movies on Spring Festival Eve was common here. The majority of the cinema-goers were young people in love.

"So you're on the go until dawn." Cui Ming gave him a cup of tea.

"Yes, I have to make a trip every thirty minutes, it's quite a job."

"Do you get extra for that?" Chai asked.

Jian laughed. "One yuan sixty! Would I miss the festival feast for that? Anyway, I'm not working for the money. By the way, would you like to go? I can get you tickets."

Cui listlessly shook his head.

Jian lit a cigarette. "I know you can't get away. You ought to prepare some snacks. There'll be a half-hour intermission after the first two shows. Let me get the cinema to announce your place is still open. I bet a lot of people will come."

"Thanks." Cui Ming immediately brightened.

"Don't be so quick to thank me, I hope you'll make something for me too."

"Sure, yours will be for nothing."

"How can I eat for nothing, I get paid extra for night shift." Jian got on his motorbike and drove off.

Listening to the fading motor, Cui Ming thought that people had become pretty careless about spending their money tonight. Why? Had they become hypnotized by Spring Festival?

The four customers asked Cui Ming to give them their bill, although it was unnecessary since they'd agreed on the price in advance. Cui Ming could see they'd eaten well—they'd polished off all the dishes.

Two famous comedians were on television.

"Would you like a little tea to cut the alcohol?" Cui Ming asked. Even before they replied, he'd gone into the kitchen to get some water. The four stayed to watch the television.

Before the water boiled, however, Jian reappeared, this time with Xiaocui riding in back.

"I bumped into Jian on my way here and got a lift." She rubbed her cheeks, which were red from the cold wind.

She was wearing a new red brocade coat and a red ribbon in her hair, and looked as though she was about to go on stage.

"What are you staring at?" She stepped back, looked down at herself and burst out laughing. "Who doesn't dress up for Spring Festival?" Then she handed Cui Ming a food container wrapped in a towel. "This is for you."

"What is it?"

"Dumplings filled with meat and shrimps. My father said they symbolize silver ingots. If you don't have dumplings on Spring Festival Eve, you won't make a fortune in the new year. So he got me to bring you some."

"You didn't have to come." Cui Ming teased her deliberately.

"What? Instead of being grateful, you complain!" She snatched the box away. "Well, I'll take it back."

"No!" Cui Ming grabbed her by the arm.

She looked down at his greasy hand but didn't try to remove it and then suddenly blushed.

Embarrassed, Cui Ming immediately let go and stuttered, "Can't you see I'm busy?"

Xiaocui looked at the water boiling. "What're you doing?"

"I'm making them some tea, because they've had a bit to drink and want to go back to work in awhile."

"It's not much good drinking tea." Her eyes twinkled. "You need to make a fruit drink. You put boiling water into a pot, add sliced apples and some haw jelly, then thicken it with starch and put some sugar in. It's got a sweet and sour taste. They'll sober up right away after drinking that." She took off her coat, put a white apron over her pink sweater and began to peel apples.

Usually, Cui Ming would have stopped her, saying, "Tea's quite enough, apples are expensive. We're in business, we have to think about profit and loss." This time he didn't, afraid he would dampen her spirits.

With Xiaocui making the drink, he could relax a bit. He leaned against the door frame watching her. Her pink jersey was shot with silver, her face and hair glowed in the dancing flame.

He'd long thought she was kindhearted, but had never found her as nice as she was tonight. Two years earlier her mother was diagnosed as having lung cancer. Cui Ming had put himself out to go to Beijing, helped her to get into a hospital and then asked his father to perform an operation. As a result, her mother lived for another year. Six months ago she'd passed away. It was just then that Cui Ming had had to leave the television university and been ditched by Bai Lin. The two blows had driven him to despair. To help him set up his restaurant, Xiaocui and her father had given up their jobs at the machine tool factory canteen and helped with the business night and day.

There were those who said that Jin had taken advantage of Cui's cafe to make a fortune, but Jin retorted, "In a couple of years, when Cui Ming can manage it all by himself, we'll go back to the canteen.

We've signed a contract with them. When he needed it, we wanted to give him whatever help we could. People ought to help one another."

During that time Jin had taught him how to cook and even asked friends to introduce girl friends, but he refused to meet them.

He wasn't clear in his own mind whether it was because of Bai Lin's behavior or for some other reason, but he just wasn't interested. All he wanted was for Jin and his daughter not to leave and to stay with him at the cafe.

"Hey, give me a hand," Xiaocui interrupted. He hadn't noticed that she had filled five bowls with the fruit mix, its sweet aroma pervading the room.

Delighted with the soup the five customers, steaming bowls in their hands, thanked her.

Red Face, impatient, took a gulp but the soup scalded his tongue. "This is the kind of thing that used to be drunk by the Empress Dowager, I suppose," he said, fanning his tongue.

"No," countered Chai, sipping noisily. "We didn't have this kind of apple then. She was out of luck."

After a few sips, Hedgehog had sobered up. "We're lucky to have this to drink tonight. Last year we could hardly get a cup of tea, never mind anything like this."

"We couldn't find anything open while we were driving," Whiskers remarked; "this is the only one."

"Yes, I've been out driving and I didn't see any others." Jian took out his cigarettes and gave them each one. "Have you heard the story of the 'Unique in the Capital' tavern? It serves steamed dumplings near Qianmen gate in Beijing."'

They all asked him to tell it.

"It was originally called the 'Li Family Tavern! Manager Li was a good man and clever at business. Every Spring Festival Eve, all the other restaurants were closed but his. He kept it open so debtors, runners and people with nowhere to go could enjoy themselves there. One year, a man in a long gown came in and said, 'I've walked all over town tonight, but only your place is open. What would you say if I called your tavern Unique in the Capital? A few days later, a sign inscribed with the name was delivered. Who do you think the man in the long gown was?"

"Who?" they chorused.

"Emperor Qian Long. And he had personally written the characters on the sign."

"Marvelous!" Red Face shouted to Cui Ming. "Your tavern's

unique too. You ought to call yours *Unique in the Capital!*"

"Oh, no!" Chai shook his head. "Li's place was in Beijing, but we're in a small town. How can we compare with the capital? What's more, it was Emperor Lian Long who named it."

"It doesn't matter whether it was the emperor or his grandmother," said Red face gesturing broadly. "In any case, the street Li's tavern was on wouldn't have been as wide as our square in front of the railway station, would it?"

"How about this?" Hedgehog paused a minute and then went on. "We're not in the capital, but next to the sea, so we could call it the *Unique by the Sea*. What do you say to that?"

"Good!" Red Face cheered. "The sea's wider than the capital anyway!"

"I'll make a new signboard for Cui," volunteered Jian. "I'll write the characters in gold on a black background to give it an antique flavor."

"Will you do a good job? It's supposed to cheer our young manager up a bit," Whiskers offered.

"Don't you worry," Xiaocui put in. "Mr. Jian does all the posters at the cinema. Making a signboard is child's play for him. Let me thank you in advance, Mr. Jian." With this she bowed to him.

Jian hurriedly stood up. "Don't thank me now, I haven't done it yet."

"Right," Red Face chimed in. "Don't be so formal. We're all friends. But we can't offer anything, only manual labor."

"From tomorrow you don't have to dump rubbish in the dustbins," Hedgehog said. "Just put it in your backyard, and we'll take it for you."

"No, thanks," Xiaocui declined. "We can take care of ourselves. The only thing is that the dustbin's a little too near the gate. If you could move it farther away, we'd be very grateful."

"Okay, we can move it to the street corner. In fact there aren't any houses there and it'll be easier for us to load," said Whiskers. "But we'd better let the boss know before we do it."

Chai started into the kitchen.

Cui Ming hurried after him. "Would you like some more soup, Chai? Let me give you some."

"No," he replied, then pointed to the back wall. "I've just been thinking. You need hot water all day long. In order to get rid of steam, I let a lot of hot water go to waste. If you can get hold of some pipes, I'll ask my chief to get them put through to the boiler. Then you can have hot water the whole winter."

Cui Ming was overjoyed at this unexpected suggestion. He took the old man's arm, "You...really are a good sort!"

"And so are those four..." Xiaocui smiled.

"Oh yes, you're a good lot, really good!" Cui Ming nodded.

On television some film stars were striking a huge bell. Outside the window fireworks exploded.

"Let's get going!" Red Face bellowed. "It's the new year, time we got back to work again."

"Wait!" Cui Ming halted, then turned to Xiaocui saying, "Warm up the dumplings in the box, quick."

"Oh, we've had more than enough," they chorused. "No more, thanks."

But Cui Ming insisted that they all sit down, "You must each be my guest and have some. Dumplings symbolize silver ingots. Eat them and you'll have good luck all year long."

Da Li is the pseudonym of Chen Yuqing and Ma Dajing. Chen was born in Shanghai in 1947. She graduated from Beijing University in 1970, worked on the editorial staff of the monthly Story Petrel *and is now a vice-chairperson of the Dalian Federation of Literary and Art Circles. Ma, a Mongolian, was born in 1947 in Nanjing. He graduated from the Chinese Department of Beijing University in 1970 and now works for the Dalian Federation. The authors have been collaborating since 1978; they have written short stories, novellas and plays. In 1983 this story won a national short story prize, and the authors became members of the Writers' Association. Song Shouquan translated the story.*

"Why didn't you tell me I'd have to work like an unpaid slave here?"

The Immigrants

BY NAIM SIDDIQUI

"I'LL change my habitat, but not my habits," Dr. Rama Rao said, before migrating to the United States, the land of his dreams.

A witty and rather eccentric man, he was about 32, and with a broad forehead, thin lips and narrow eyes looking magnified by thick glasses, he had a look of professional efficiency. Light-skinned, short in stature, he was a dedicated medical man, for six days in the week. On Sunday, he used to play bridge the whole day, and drink beer almost all the time, without getting drunk—or so he thought. On such occasions his talk became brilliant, even philosophical sometimes.

"As a dentist," he once said, "I belong to the underclass of the medical profession. Underclass! But we are the people who attend to our patients from the cradle to the grave."

"That's only a cliché," said Kabeer, one of his friends and bridge partners.

"It is not a cliché," he exclaimed. "Look here, what's human life on earth except a journey from toothlessness to toothlessness? And we are the people who—" He paused for effect.

"—who provide the false teeth, the partials, the dentures and who fill the cavities," Kabeer interposed.

"You are no dentist, but you are the greatest defender of faith in the dental profession," Dr. Rama Rao remarked, relishing the sarcasm.

Before migrating to the United States, Dr. Rama Rao lived in Bombay, in a small flat (apartment) in a narrow lane in the Bhaindi Bazaar area. He had a small clinic on the second floor of a building which had apartments on the ground floor. The building opposite had a rather dubious signboard: "Tutorial Institute for Girls." It didn't seem to have any classrooms, and on its ground floor was a small cheap hotel. Dr. Rao had a 15-year old Ambassador car, which was more temperamental than he was.

"My car needs manpower as well as horsepower," he often used to say. "But this is Bombay. There's plenty of manpower here for my car: beggars, street urchins, jobless laborers. Yes, Bombay, the world capital of the homeless, has no lack of manpower for my old car."

While driving in the streets of Bombay he often became irritated. "Too many people here," he once told Kabeer, "and too many types of vehicles from the time the wheel was invented to the present day. And then those suicidal pedestrians and old, abandoned cows and buffaloes meditating right in the middle of the street! More than seven hundred million people! Where did they all come from?"

"Is that a rhetorical question?" Kabeer asked.

"They all came from the Gateway of India. I say, close down the Gateway of India for at least a few years."

"Don't be obscene," Kabeer remarked.

"Obscene? What can be more obscene than a woman producing a brood of twelve children? If the fertility of our women could be transferred to our soil, all our problems would be solved."

But he was not really a misogynist. And he couldn't be. His wife, Sarojini, (Saroj, as he called her) was petite and pretty. Everything about her was small, with two exceptions. With her firm, rather large breasts (large for her size), a narrow waist and slightly large, very shapely hips, she looked like one of those famous paintings in Ajanta. As for her age, no one could tell it for certain. She could be 22; she could be 29. She herself was rather confused about it.

To reach the land of his dreams, Dr. Rama Rao had to keep himself busy for about a year. His elder brother, who was now a U.S. citizen and lived in California, had sponsored him and his wife. They both had to get international passports, police clearance certificates, "No Objection" certificates, Income Tax clearance certificates and medical reports. Then the interview and the long wait for the visa.

"This is the beginning of a new life for us," Dr. Rao told his wife when at last, after all the confusion at Bombay airport, they found themselves firmly seated in a plane.

Saroj seemed to be lost in thought. "Don't you feel sorry for leaving our people behind?" she asked, with a sad, tired look. Her parents and a sister lived in Bombay. The leave-taking at the airport had been a touching scene. Her eyes were still red.

"You'll be meeting your people soon," he reassured her. "We're not leaving forever. How can we forget our people and our motherland?"

When they reached Frankfurt and changed planes, Saroj began to feel a little better. When at last they landed at J.F.K. International Airport, Dr. Rama Rao was quite excited.

"Have you got anything to declare?" the Customs woman asked.

"No cocaine, no heroin, no marijuana," Dr. Rao said.

She smiled. "Anything else?"

"Nothing. Here are the keys. See for yourself."

She didn't. Then their most important stop was at the Immigration Office in the Terminal Building for their Green Cards. When Dr. Rao and his wife were asked to have their fingerprints taken, he could not check his humor. "We have no police record, officer," he said. "This is the first time that we are having our fingerprints taken. I hope it's also the last."

Then they rushed to take the flight to Los Angeles International Airport.

In Southern California, Dr. Rama Rao's elder brother, Narsimha Rao (Narsy, as he was called) lived in a three-bedroom house in Villa Park. He was about 12 years older than Rama Rao; light-skinned, short, with a thinning scalp, thick glasses and a little paunch.

At the airport the two brothers met with Asian exuberance. Their wives met with more courtesy than warmth. Narsy's wife, Renuka (Renu, as everybody called her) was tall, slim, with a face more angular than oval. She had visited Bombay with her husband about five years earlier, to attend Rama Rao's wedding. She remembered Saroj as a bride—wrapped up in a red and gold brocaded sari, bejeweled from head to foot, and covered with garlands on the wedding day. Now Saroj looked less gorgeous and more curvaceous.

Rama Rao grabbed his brother's two children.

"Oh! Is it Padma?" he almost shouted. "You've grown into a big girl, but—but you're getting very old. You're losing your teeth."

Padma's partly toothless smile amused him.

"Ask Uncle to fix them," Renu said.

"Oh no," Rama Rao said. "Nature will fix them first. My turn will come next.".

Padma's younger brother, Suresh, was about three years old, and seemed a little confused and rather frightened at first by his uncle's excessive warmth.

Narsy was an engineer, and Renu worked as a computer programmer. Padma was now in Grade 3. Narsy used to take little Suresh to a baby-sitter in the neighborhood on his way to his job, and pick him up on the way back home.

Much of the first week was quite exciting for the new arrivals. They visited the usual places—Disneyland, the Wax Museum, Universal Studios, North Berry Farm, et cetera.

"We'll go to San Diego next weekend," Narsy said with a vague touch of finality. That touch of finality was always subject to his wife's approval. "Monday to Friday we have no time. We have to work like dogs."

Dogs don't work—do they? Rama Rao thought, but did not say so. He had too much respect for his elder brother to contradict him and called him *bhayya* (title of respect for an elder brother).

"Don't you remember?" Renu asked her husband. "Next Saturday we have a dinner party at Kamla's, followed by a musical evening. It'll be a big party. They have invited two good singers and a *tabla* player."

"What about Sunday?" Narsy asked tentatively.

"Don't you know we'll return home very late at night? Do you want to doze off while driving on Sunday?"

Whenever Narsy and his wife expected to return late from a party, they always used to call a baby-sitter for their children. But now it was different. Saroj was there to look after the children.

Kamla's dinner party was the usual scene of profusion, confusion and overcrowding, of paper plates bending under the weight of roast chicken, *biryani, shish kebab, samosas,* etc. All the ladies squatted in the family room after dinner for the musical performance. So did the men, in the drawing room.

One of the two singers did not turn up. The one who did, was an amateur, a student at UCLA. With him came a *tabla* player. The amateur sang some famous *gazals* by Ghalib, Zafar, Faiz and others, and some popular Hindi film songs. And while the men listened, the women talked most of the time.

On Sunday, the first thing Rama Rao remembered was the promise he had made to himself. What he missed most was his bridge party. As for the beer, well, he could have plenty of it and drink in solitude. But drinking in solitude is morbid, he thought, and drinking in the presence of his elder brother was very bad manners. Only very liberated Indians permitted it, and the two brothers were by no means liberated. In fact, they came from a family of orthodox Hindu Brahmins who were vegetarians. But Narsy had to leave his vegetarianism at home, and Rama Rao knew he would have to do the same.

"Do you play bridge now?" Rama Rao ventured to ask his brother who had just finished his breakfast at about 11 a.m. "You used to play bridge in Bombay, you remember?"

"Bridge?" Narsy asked. "Who has the time to play bridge here? At least, I don't. I know you're a bridge bum. I'll try to find some idlers about town who can—"

"—Who can what?" Renu interrupted. She had just stepped out of her bedroom.

"Nothing," Narsy said in a conciliatory tone. "We were talking about bridge. But, Ramu, first things first. Let's discuss your plans here. Your plans. First you have to pass the entrance exam—ECFMG, or whatever it's called."

"Yes, I know."

"You have to get good grades, remember," Narsy continued rather pontifically (his wife was listening), "and then to get your D.D.S. you have to apply for residency. You have to look for a job, too. When I first came here and was doing my M.S., I was doing two part-time jobs until my graduation—all kinds of odd jobs."

"Hello, Saroj," Renu said very sweetly when she saw her coming up with Suresh. "Narsy, you see how much she likes our Suresh, and how much attached to her he already feels! Now we don't have to take him to the baby-sitter and coop him up the whole day in a stranger's house. Dear Saroj can look after him so well! What do you say, Saroj?"

Saroj, a woman of few words but not few emotions, smiled a little. "I think that'll be fine," she said.

Renu did not add that it would mean a saving of more than $300 a month.

Dr. Rama Rao soon became an ardent reader of classified ads in the *Los Angeles Times* and *Orange County Register*. Transportation was the first problem. Narsy often dropped him at the nearest bus stop. He soon mastered the OCTD timetable and enjoyed the rides for some time. His favorite stops were those at Mall of Orange and the bus terminus at Sixth and Flower Street in Santa Ana.

"This must be a leisured society, judging by the frequency of the buses," he once said. "And what a variety of people here! Aliens from all over the world! Why doesn't somebody write a book on the *Browning of America?*"

But he soon got tired of the long wait and the boredom of transfers from one bus to another, and he decided to buy a car—a used car, of course. He had never driven a really big car in India; so, with Narsy's approval, he bought an old Pontiac Bonneville.

"This car has more length than the room we are in now," he said. "If we are thrown out, we can live in the car."

Then came his first invitation. It was from Narsy's friend, Dixit, a prosperous, pot-bellied businessman from Orange County. In a large gathering of businessmen, doctors, engineers, accountants and managers, et cetera (all Indians), Rama Rao found himself reduced to a total nonentity. Narsy introduced him to his close friends, some of whom glanced at him with a "so-you-are-the-country-cousin" look. "You have just come from Bombay?" one of them asked. "What's the latest scandal in Indian politics?"

"I'm not interested in politics or scandals," Rama Rao said. "I'm only interested in the tooth, the whole tooth, and nothing but the tooth."

Some ignored him; others laughed. One of them said, with the air of a minor humorist, "You can make an excellent witness." Another man came forward and said, "Let me see, I think we should coin a new word for what you've just said. What about—what about 'dento-centric'? You have a 'dento-centric' view of life—centered on the teeth."

"Excellent," Rama Rao said. "Do you teach English?"

"I'm afraid I do," he replied.

"I narrowly escaped becoming a teacher of English myself," Rama Rao said. "Father didn't like it; so I became a dentist."

"Out of the frying pan into the fire," the same humorist remarked.

Not so funny, Rama Rao thought.

Saroj, sitting among the ladies, was ignored, too, even by Renu, and was made to feel that she had come from a primitive world into the center of civilization.

Baby-sitting, cooking, washing and cleaning were now Saroj's daily chores. Renu had no time for housekeeping and paid very little attention to her children. Rama Rao was busy job hunting and studying for his exams. He had mailed more than one hundred copies of his resumé and had several interviews.

One evening, on his return home, he was surprised to find Saroj in bed.

"What's wrong?" he asked.

"Everything," she said, sobbing. "I can't stand it any more. Looking after the baby the whole day, doing all the cooking, washing and cleaning. I can't do it any more. Why didn't you tell me I'd have to work like an unpaid slave here?"

There were tears in her dark eyes. Rama Rao knew this would happen one day. He didn't try to defend his sister-in-law.

"But what can we do?" he asked.

"Let's leave this place and rent a flat."

"Renting an apartment is not so easy, my dear," he said. "What about the expense—the rent, utilities, et cetera?"

"But I can get a job," she replied. "After all, with my Bachelor's degree I should be able to get one."

"But what they ask for here is local job experience, and you don't have any."

At this gloomy prospect she began to sob again. With tears in her eyes, her innocent-looking face looked more beautiful. Her low-cut nightgown exposed her shapely breasts.

Tired and unsure of himself, Rama Rao thought, Saroj's problem is the problem of many other women: overused by day, underused by night.

At last Rama Rao passed the entrance exam, and spent about a week in getting ready his applications for residency. He also got a job as Dental Assistant in a small dentistry.

Now that Rama Rao was in a position to move into an apartment, Renu's treatment of Saroj softened a good deal. But Saroj was determined to move out.

"You should start looking for a flat now," she told her husband. "I can't waste my time like this here any more."

"So you want to waste it in an apartment?" Rama Rao said.

He politely introduced the subject to his brother, who tentatively agreed. "But ask Renu, he said. "I don't know what she thinks about it."

He did know, of course. She didn't like the idea at all, but couldn't persuade Saroj to change her mind.

They moved into a small apartment in Fullerton with their scanty belongings. Rama Rao was very happy. "This is the second phase in a new life for us," he said. "Now I can be myself. Now I can play bridge and drink beer with my friends the whole day on Sundays."

"What about your bridge partners?" Saroj asked.

"I have them already," Rama Rao said. "You'll see them all on Sunday."

And on Sunday morning they did turn up—a motley group. Gopal was about forty, a short, fat man with an ungainly mustache and rather bad teeth. He was a small businessman in Orange County. Srivasthava was an engineer—middle-aged, with unremarkable features except for his large bulging eyes. The third man was Hameed. He was working for his Master's degree in Mechanical Engineering. He was tall, had an athletic figure (without really being an athlete), sharp features and thick hair. He was by no means a good bridge player but Rama Rao believed he could improve fast.

No one drank much beer except Rama Rao. They played the whole day, with a rather hurried lunch, until dinnertime. Saroj was a spectator, as usual. It was a rather dull game for her, but she was wondering who the attractive young man was, wasting his time on an unexciting game.

Saroj started her job hunting. She mailed dozens of resumés, and received as many polite letters of rejection. At last, she got a part-time job as an assistant in a library—twenty hours a week, Tuesday through Thursday.

The Sunday sessions continued. Saroj's main interest was in glancing furtively at the young player. Their eyes often met—a combination of shyness and occasional daring.

Then on one Sunday Hameed came rather late. His battered old car had given him some trouble on the way.

"You may have trouble with your car again on your way back," Rama Rao told him after dinner. "And if you're stalled on the dark freeway, you won't know what to do. So stay here and return tomorrow after giving some first-aid to your car."

The next morning Rama Rao rushed to his work as usual, and when Hameed got up, he found Saroj routinely, but more eagerly busy in the kitchen.

"I have work today in the afternoon," Hameed said casually.

She looked up. A thrill went down her spine.

"You said you're sharing an apartment with a friend," she said, "do you know much about cooking?"

"Not much, really. I cook some rice, minced meat, and one or two other things. And of course I know how to make tea."

"I'll make some *samosas* and some sweets for you," she said with eager eyes.

"Thanks a lot, but not today."

"Next week, then," she said.

"It's so sweet of you, Saroj," he said. "You—you don't know how kind-hearted you are and how beautiful."

Conversation turned into warm whispers. He could hardly believe that her beautiful body, with its voluptuous curves, was now in his firm grip. She felt exhilaration and then some remorse. But it was exhilaration that triumphed each time they continued to meet.

Life, mundane life, went on as before. Rama Rao at last acquired those three letters—D.D.S.—and felt himself closer to the realization of his immigrant's dream.

Born in 1940, in Hyderabad, India, Naim Siddiqui was educated in India, and at Oxford where he earned a Master's degree in English language and literature. He has taught in India, Liberia and other countries. His short stories, criticism and poetry have been published. He is now working on a novel.

"Here it's love that matters, not lineage, and the last thing one thinks of is marriage within the clan or family."

Walls

BY AMNON SHAMOSH

ONE brother fell in love with Tel Aviv. Tel Aviv in those days, the mid-1930's, was a fresh young maiden, her face to the future, a gentle sea breeze caressing her golden hair and swirling her skirt around her thighs. Whoever saw her was captivated by her charm and promise: the reviving Hebrew on her crimson lips and the vision of a new society in her heart, and her legs, bronzed by sun and sea, striding swiftly toward the morrow. Sandals on her feet and a kerchief on her head, she had but few yesterdays, and none before these, and all her thoughts she fixed on the new day dawning after a long night.

Not so Jerusalem, whom his older brother loved and where he built his home. Jerusalem was a cherished old grandmother, adorned with God's grace. Her hair was silver and her forehead grooved, the wisdom of the ages shone from eyes whose beauty the years had not dimmed. Her gait was unhurried, her steps measured, as if she knew from where she came and where she meant to go. Her body was all wrinkles and folds, each concealing a rich past where glory and ruin, ebb and flow, dwelled one with the other, one on top of the other. And even if a man could plummet the depths of one wrinkle, the rest—shrouding themselves in mystery and enfolding countless riddles—eluded him. A venerable old lady, Jerusalem was, who, having endured all that she had as well as she had, could look to a fine future.

Aharon, who was the first of his family in Aleppo, Syria, to settle in Eretz Israel (Land of Israel), was dazzled by the fast-moving pace of the City of Work and Creation. The burst of construction and the *joie de vivre* that were Tel Aviv in those days seduced and conquered him. The breezes coming from the West ruffled his hair, and the ivory comb which he had brought from home and which at first had never left his pocket, now lay in the shower he shared with three other bachelors. He saw the tanned faces with the look that said "Forward!" He lowered his gaze to the short khaki pants and the muscular legs marching toward a clear goal, and he said to himself, "I'm with you."

Here, in little Tel Aviv between Ha-Aliyah Street and Meshek Ha-Poalot, he found the change he was looking for. Not a city of many nations like the one he left behind, no convergence here of every people and tongue, no tense and menacing dwelling together of Arab and Jew—Tel Aviv was an all-Jewish city, all-Hebrew, all waiting to build and to be built. "Today you are moving on to a new land"—so Bialik had said on *Shabbat* (Saturday) in Ohel Shem.

What could be better than this: *Shabbat* eve in socialist fellowship, songs which unite hearts, the outpouring of a concertina and girls dancing; and on *Shabat* morning the cool sea and the scorching sand, girls lounging, and a bite of freedom in the salt air; and later, during the *Oneg Shabbat* (a partaking of food after services), the Eastern lilt of Hebrew and a piano playing Western airs, and harmony between *casquette* and beret and a bare head; and a *Shabbat* meal at the cooperative restaurant, so different from Mother's cooking, free of yesterday's aromas and of diaspora's prayers, and across from you a burly labor leader sits down with a tired groan, one of the Lamed-Vav (36 saintly people) who waited on line with the others for space at the table and now he eats with you and like you with a simplicity that tugs at the heart.

There is a "first" about Tel Aviv. The first Hebrew city in the world. And Aharon acquired a "first" in it—if not to say primogeniture, which is a concept whose time has passed—by being first in his family to settle there, thereby paving the way for the others to follow suit. From the day he first knew what's what he used to envy his older brother, Shlomo, seeking—knowingly or unknowingly—to surpass and outstrip him. When Shlomo-Salomon gained importance, even leadership, in the community, Aharon began to think of leaving home. Came a gust of wind from Zion and turned his leaving into aliyah (immigrating and becoming a citizen of Eretz Israel)—what's more admirable than aliyah? Soon ecstatic letters began to arrive accompanied with photographs: one on the steps of the Mugrabi Opera House, one atop the Casino-by-the-sea, one at the Seven Mills on the Yarkon River, another at the gate of Ha-Vaad Ha-Poel on Allenby Street, and in all of them our "Haron" standing tall and earnest, his hair disheveled and his smile sure—pictures which provoked interest and respect and arguments without end.

What an opera was, or a casino, people knew—our town was no province, God forbid. But Ha-Vaad Ha-Poel (an organization within the Labor Party) was a real puzzle, which none among us could solve. At any rate, it was a large building and our "Haron," who began to sign his letters Aharon, found himself a job there—all power to him. This job of his took him to Ha-Bayit Ha-Adom and Ha-Bayit Ha-Kahol and Beit Ha-Halutzot—names whose Hebrew covered up their strangeness, and which were finally accepted with raised eyebrows and a nod of the head. But the childish things he wrote about "family wages" at the Histadrut were received with a wink and a shrug. The boy is naïve, even a fool. The Yemenite tea-attendant—so the silly boy wrote—receives higher wages than does his Ashkenazi boss, because the boss has one child while the Yemenite has many. It is not right, this, not the way of the world; certainly not the way of the Ashkenazim, of whom we've heard a thing or two.

Said his mother to Salomon her eldest: "Go see what your little brother is up to in that Jewish city which, were it not for rumors of meat mixing with milk in her restaurants—may my lips not sin—I would call the City of Messiah Ben Yosef." He smiled and asked, "Ben Yosef?" She said, "I'm surprised at you, ya bni (my son). Messiah Ben David has but one city, Jerusalem, there is no other. The son nodded his head in agreement, then started to plan, to prepare, and to pack for his journey.

His father called him to his sick bed and told him: "You're going to scout the land, my son, to find a home for the family whose fate now rests on your shoulders. I know that my days are numbered and I take comfort in the knowledge that I won't be here to burden you as you move to the Holy Land."

Said the son: "Don't say that, Father. Surely you'll be with us when we enter Jerusalem's gates, and Inshallah (God willing)..."

But the father interrupted: "Don't speak words you don't believe in your heart, not to your father! And know, my son, that I'm not complaining. Our Patriarch Moses did not merit entering the land of Israel, and who am I that I should merit it?"

He stopped speaking, lost in thought, and a heavy silence hung between Father and Son, until the door opened and Mother entered, a small pad in her hand: "Write a note," she said to her husband, "for our son to slip between the stones of the Wailing Wall. Everything's ready."

At his mother's behest Salomon stopped in Tsfat to light a candle at Shimon Bar Yohai's and in Tiberias to give alms at Rabbi Meir Baal Haness's—both for his ailing father who had not left his bed all that year. Then he boarded a bus and, traveling for many hours among the citrus groves, finally he came to Tel Aviv.

Here his eyes opened wide and his heart hovered between marvel and recoil, between wonder and excitement and between misgiving and doubt. A Jewish policeman in uniform directing traffic at Kikar Ha-Moshavot is a heartwarming, thrilling sight, downright the At'halta Degeula (Aramaic for the beginning of the redemption); were he of an older generation he would have recited the *Sheheheyanu* (prayer of thanks). But dignitaries, doctors, and directors in short pants and rolled-up sleeves, no deference or decorum, no jacket and no tie—it's nothing short of laxity and adolescence, a plain lack of good taste. The letters of *Sidur* and *Humash* beckoning from signs on every street corner—a sight for sore eyes and a joy for the heart. But the same holy letters rolling in the streets or thrust into trash cans—a sacrilege and a great shame. A girl on the beach in a robe and sandals shedding both to tan herself—a comely sight, acceptable too, even if it does arouse and unsettle mere mortals. But those girls who sit across from you in offices, their legs crossed, their skirts hiked up, their necklines low, their naked toes wriggling at you like restless fish—it distracts and corrupts, even vexes and revolts. No modesty and no class. They're playing with fire, tempting the Devil. And this sweaty and arousing rubbing of bodies in the packed buses of Ha-Maavir. And the constant exposure to the beating sun. And the constant insane rush which suits neither the temperament nor the climate.

Had it not been for Jerusalem, which showed him a different face, it's doubtful that he would have come to Israel to stay. After several days of small quarrels and larger misunderstandings Salomon said to Aharon his brother: "I've seen all that your Tel Aviv has to offer." And he added, "I'll be back in four or five days—maybe."

Our friend went up to Jerusalem and rented a small room for himself in a pine-shaded pension in Rehavia. He found to his glee, that Europe had sent here not only the daughters of mischievous Warsaw but those of Berlin, Vienna, and Prague as well, with their hats and gloves and parasols, their curtsies and thank-yous. The sting of the bee he did not feel in this his first short visit, only the honey of good manners, which he relished. Men walked about properly dressed, in hats and neckties, and their ladies on their arms, wearing dresses of organdy with collars and sleeves. The former tipped their hats one to the other while the latter pulled off their gloves with their fingers and stretched out their hands to be kissed. Their manners were all graceful and their conversations genteel.

Every morning Shlomo sat in a fine cafe leafing through

newspapers held in bamboo frames. At noon he dined at the pension, a white napkin spread on his knees, and engraved silverware in his hands. In the evening he sat at the Cafe Vienna sipping café au lait, gazing at the mixture of East and West streaming down Yafo Street like an endless bankless river. Those three places were within walking distance one from the other, a Jerusalem-type walk which takes in the smell of the East, the rhythm of the East, the spirit of the East.

The East at its best, he would muse to himself on his way from the Cafe Vienna to Jaafar's Cafe, which lies just inside the Damascus Gate, blends here with the West at its best. Or, on second thought: meets here and...will blend in time. And another thought: a meeting of equals, equal in value though markedly different in essence. And when he sat down at Jaafar's and swallowed some cold water to wash out the sweet taste of the *kenafeh* he looked out the window and thought to himself: Some day I might look into the link between people's way of walking and their way of life.

By the time he set out for Aviv Taxi Service to return to his brother's home he knew that Jerusalem would be his city soon *(Inshallah!)* and the other—his brother's city.

"Taxi? Why a taxi?" his brother wondered.

"One bus trip was enough. Crowds and perspiration are not my cup of tea."

A real bourgeois, thought Aharon to himself, using terms he had learned here. A snob. Pampered. Buses aren't good enough for him, the big shot. Squandering what little money was left to the family after Father's long years of labor, as if it were his own.

Aloud he said, "Come, let's go home and get something to eat."

Answered Shlomo, *"Yallah!"* (Let's go!) And then he added, smiling, "This Hebrew which is reviving itself has quite an appetite. It swallows up Arab words without leaving a trace, e.g., *yallah, mabsut, ala-kefak, ahalan, dahilak, dugri*."

Aharon smiled in return, looking for something to say which would not sound argumentative. They walked in silence, knowing that whatever subject they broached was bound to end in disagreement.

Shlomo walked and thought to himself, I wonder if he knows how angry Father was at his leaving. He up and went just as our troubles descended on us: Father's illness, the sudden loss of income, Mother's tears, the little one's fears...

And Aharon's gaze traveled from his brother's tasteful little leather suitcase to the shining kidskin shoes on his feet. He remembered how Shlomo had yelled to their mother in the kitchen: "Let him go! We don't need him! He never was one to help shoulder a load. Always managed to shirk his responsibilities." And Mother's whisper which was barely audible through the door: "But you, Salomon *rohi* (my soul), you never wanted to share any responsibility with him." And his impudent brother's loud response, which even a deaf man could hear: "Because I know him. He is incapable of sharing. To take—yes. To share—never. Always been his own man."

"You know, the new Hebrew borrowed from Yiddish also," Aharon said.

"That Yiddish..." Shlomo hissed, and said no more.

They climbed up the stairs, Aharon in front, humming to himself, "Tamar, don't you worry/Mother knows already," his keys ready in his hand. Shlomo came behind him, holding the suitcase in his left hand and pulling on the railing with the right, puzzling over the strange names on the door—Hebrew letters in foreign combinations: Stieglitz, Sokolovsky, Weingarten, Sharfstein.

"Sit down," said Aharon, "I'll see what's in the ice-box."

He called it an ice-box this time, thought Shlomo. *Maalesh* (good). As long as he doesn't call it a refrigerator—the way he did the first day when he showed him around the apartment, a quarter of whose shares he owns.

"Will you drink something cold from the ice-box?"

"Whatever you have. Only not *gazoz* (soda)."

The word *gazoz* Shlomo pronounced with exaggerated scorn, wondering himself what sort of demon got into him.

"Cold water, then?"

"Let it be water. 'Blessed are Thou...by Whose word all things exist.' "

"Something to eat?"

"Bring out Mother's *ma'mul*. I was thinking of home and I could almost taste Mother's *ma'mul*."

"No more *ma'mul*, sorry. My girlfriend was here when you were in Jerusalem; she wanted to meet you. She polished off the *ma'mul*, and I helped her."

"Your girlfriend? Your fiancée or something? 'Polished off—that's nice. And where have you been hiding her?"

"She was in a kibbutz, in some seminar of Ha-Noar Ha-Oved. Got back the day before yesterday, and first thing she asked about you."

"*Salamta* (Peace be with you). Asked about me."

There was tension in the air as the one brother sat drumming with his fingers on the plastic tablecloth covering the wooden table and occasionally beating out the rhythm with his right knee, while the other ran to and fro bringing dishes to the table with a distracted look and an unsteady hand.

"A girlfriend? What's the hurry? *Istanna ya gdeesh! hitta yitla' el hashish.*" (Tarry a while, O horse/until the grass grows.)

"If you wish, she's more than a girlfriend. But that's what they call it here, girlfriend. And there's no hurry. Although it's quite serious."

"You were always serious. I wouldn't be surprised if even here you'll jump ahead of me."

Aharon got up from the table, as though avoiding an excessive closeness which would end up in a quarrel. As host he felt it his duty to minimize friction. He tried to say something though he was still chewing. He began to cough, a cough which grew worse and which forced him finally to withdraw to the bathroom to rinse his face with cold water. Shlomo waited for him deep in thought, his knee spread apart, his hands clasped together between them.

If I could tell Father and Mother myself, Aharon thought, they'd swallow this, maybe even be glad for it. Father deserves to see his sons married in his lifetime. But this messenger-mediator Salomon with his fickle tongue—that's all I need.

Where is she from and what's her extraction? thought Shlomo

in turn. He won't tell me unless I ask him. "She asked about you."
If she asked about me, I can ask about her, no?

"And is she...*min ginisna*, one of us?"

Here Aharon burst into relieved laughter, surprising his brother
who failed to see the joke.

"This is Eretz Israel, ya Salomon, not Halab."

"What do you mean?"

"Here no one asks where you're from." (No one asks because
one knows without asking, thought Shlomo to himself, holding
back his tongue). "Here it's love that matters, not lineage, and the
last thing one thinks of is marriage within the clan or family." (Hey,
watch out! You're approaching the danger zone!)

"You didn't answer my question."

"She's Yemenite."

Shlomo made every effort to hide his reaction to the news, but
surprise and dismay were plainly written on his face. Had he heard
"Ashkenazia" he could not have been more shaken. Yes, his
brother was capable of everything.

These shriveled and guttural Yemenites aroused in Shlomo a
certain liking mixed with contempt. The men with their curled
sidelocks and the women in their colorful clothing—dress on top of
trousers, like the Muslim maids, for example, who used to come to
us from remote and primitive villages—fed his feelings of
superiority, which lately had been starved. From the day he arrived
they captured his curiosity, though not his heart. He looked down
on their accent and dark skin, their dress and food. What anyone
saw in *melawah* and *jahnun* (spicy Yemenite food) he could never
understand. He turned up his nose at their tin can drumming. Both
their *ayin* and *het* (letters in the alphabet) and the hot pepper in
their food he found excessive. What this brother of his, this
unworthy son of their father, saw in a daughter of Yemen, Shlomo
could not understand. At least if she were Egyptian, from Tunis,
Turkey, or Greece—but Yemen?

Said Aharon to his brother, "What time do you have? Six? At
seven she'll meet us by the clock. She's dying to meet you. We'll
go to some cafe. When you get to know her you'll see why I'm
crazy about her."

Shlomo already knew that "the clock" was the square graceless clock near the Mugrabi Opera, where young Tel Avivians often met. His brother admired the clock and its modern shape just as he loved the tasteless hot dogs sold nearby by the Ashkenazi vendor with the white paper cap saying "Grab a bite." According to the neophyte Tel Avivian the ancient clock gracing Bab-al-Faraj was old-fashioned and too ornate. Even that almost caused them to fight. And this manner of speaking of his: "dying to meet you," "crazy about her"—these expressions sprang up in the sands. Me, Shlomo thought, I'd rather have Jerusalem's walls than Tel Aviv's sands.

And Aharon thought to himself: If I tell him the whole truth, that she dances with the Beit Ha-Halutzot dance troupe and that she also sings—he's sure to explode. Where we come from "dancer" is practically a synonym for "prostitute." A dancer who also sings, and a Yemenite to boot—better stick with half-truths now, there's time for details later.

And more: His attitude toward the Yemenites reflects a strange mix. They seem to remind him of an aspect of himself, a dark aspect of which he is ashamed and from which he wants to flee. They project the Arab and the Eastern in themselves openly, without shame, and that confounds Salomon. For him, the East in him comes cloaked in Parisian finery, made to order clothes, *haute couture*. We have 50 minutes left. What shall we talk about?

"And how did you like Jerusalem?"

"More beautiful than I expected. Surpasses the imagination."

"Did you see everything? Did you go to the Wall? Did you climb up the mountains to get a good view?"

"I slipped Father's note between the stones of the Western Wall, and my own note—an oral note—I left between the stones of the Eastern Wall...of the Hebrew University on Mt. Scopus." And suddenly in a burst of candor puzzling even to himself Shlomo laid bare before his brother the storm in his heart. "I went up to Mt. Scopus. I sat in the shade and gazed at the Temple Mount spread out before me. A light Western breeze was blowing on my face; across from me, through stylized arches, the great Eastern domes shimmered in the sun. Behind me I sensed the desert which comes up here and meets man's deeds and works for lo these three thousand years. I felt that this is the place and this is the time for the Western culture of Magnes and Buber to meet the Eastern culture of Musa El Alami and Taha Husayn and the Nashashibites, for that of the Baal Shem Tov to meet that of Rabbi Joseph Caro—a meeting of mutual respect and fruitful cross-fertilization. Rehavia and Sheikh Jerakh, Beit Ha-Kerem and Talbieh—they could not live one with the other without influencing one another."

How naïve he is, Aharon thought. And bombastic. Western humanism driven to Eastern exaggeration.

"Things look different when you live in their midst," he said almost in a whisper, choosing his words, "when you look at people and problems from up close, not from the mountain tops..."

"Only from a mountain top can you see the whole, the ensemble. Maybe this is why I fell in love with Jerusalem; it's surrounded by mountains."

"You look down from up there and you think nothing separates Western Jewish Rehavia from Eastern Arab Talbieh (which is eyeing the West) from the Eastern Jewish territories. Go down and mix with the people—in their eyes and hearts you'll see walls."

And to himself he said, "I'm beginning to talk like him. Maybe it's catching."

Staring at his brother's smart summer suit Aharon absent-mindedly tucked the tails of his shirt back into his khaki trousers. He wanted to say to his brother, the dreamer, Magnes and El Alami have hardly any influence. Buber is still in Germany and Taha Husain in Cairo, and the powers-that-be are moving toward a head-on collision. And if even you and I can't manage to...

The door that flew open interrupted his thoughts. A neighbor, returning from work, burst in shaken and pale, and without a greeting asked, "Did you hear the news?" And when they said "No," he told them that three Jewish buses had been attacked in various parts of the country and that dozens of casualties were reported.

"I'm afraid we're in for it now," Aharon murmured.

"And you, my friend," said the neighbor, "still call the Arabs 'cousins'?"

"I don't understand..." Shlomo said, and he stood up.

 *Short story writer, novelist and poet, Amnon Shamosh is one of Israel's most prolific writers and a prominent figure in the new wave of writers from Oriental countries. He has won the Prime Minister's Award for Creativity and the Jerusalem Agnon Prize for Literature. Mr. Shamosh was born in Syria in 1929 and arrived in Israel in 1938. He is a founding member of Kibbutz Maayan-Baruk. Nili Wachtel translated the story.*

"Every day I counted the days until Suguru's return."

Delayed Homecoming

BY TERUKO HYUGA

"MOMOKO, we must go home for *Obon* (the time the spirits of the departed return to be with their families). We didn't go for the New Year's holidays," Suguru said.

"I know but I don't feel well," I said. "I get trainsick, and it's worse in summer. Wait until September. Please! That's just one month. Write to your mother that we'll come to see her in September. She'll understand."

"It's cooler there in summer," Suguru said, "and it's two months delay because we have *Obon* in July, not in August."

"July! We can't leave now! Haruo doesn't like a long train trip in summer," I said. "Please! I'm not ready to leave!"

"It doesn't sound logical to want to stay in hot Tokyo during the summer and not want to get away to Northern Japan. My mother may think we are just making excuses...If we can't go now, we must promise to go in September and go without fail," Suguru said.

"Yes. I promise!" I said. "I'm sorry."

"That's all right. It's just that I feel guilty," he said.

"I know. I am sorry. I feel guilty, too," I said. "But we'll make it up to her!"

I really felt awful about this. When Suguru and I had married in Tokyo five years ago, we had promised his widowed mother that we would come to live with her as soon as possible. Now Haruo, our son, was four and we were still living in Tokyo...all because of me. Of course, my parents, relatives and friends were happy to have us in Tokyo. But Suguru and I had managed to visit his mother only once a year thus far. Last year he tried to persuade me to go at the end of the year so that we could spend the New Year's holidays with her but I was too terrified to go to the northern tip of Honshu Island in winter.

"All right," Suguru said and wrote to his mother. I knew he wished he didn't have to write that letter.

Suguru's mother responded right away, saying that she was looking forward to having us all in September and that she was fine.

We spent *Obon* with my parents, and my guilt feeling grew as I watched my parents surrounded by all their children and their children's families. Suguru was an only son and his mother was alone.

"Can we leave on September 1?" Suguru said in mid-August, the train schedule in his hands.

"Yes," I said.

I knew early September could still be very warm but I had to acknowledge and respond to Suguru's and his mother's feelings.

Sometime after lunch on August 21, a telegram arrived. I opened and read it. It said Suguru's mother had died. I read it again and again and again. My mind went blank. Like a robot, I called Suguru at his office. When I finished reading the telegram, he said nothing for a long while.

"I'll come home as soon as possible. We have to leave tonight. Start packing right now, Momoko," he said.

"Yes," I said, with a throbbing heart.

I was very upset. Because of me, he hadn't gone to spend *Obon* with his mother. I wished we had all gone! I packed our funeral clothes and Haruo's clothes. I called my parents and explained. My mother wanted to come to help me but I declined because by the time she arrived we might be gone.

We took a special night express train. Suguru didn't speak. He kept his eyes closed. I knew what he was thinking. He should have gone to see his mother for the New Year's holidays; he should have moved to live with her; he should have gone in July. He was blaming himself. I felt just terrible. It was all my fault. Because of me, he was now blaming himself. I knew he was more angry with himself than with me. I wanted to apologize but if I said anything, we might fight, cry...He might say it's too late now. And it was too late now to apologize.

The train arrived at our destination early in the morning. As we walked to his mother's home, many times I almost said I was sorry...

"Will you forgive me?" I finally said when the house came in sight.

He looked at me and nodded his head once. I knew it didn't mean he had blamed me but had forgiven me. He just couldn't talk. I realized more strongly than ever that I had been a selfish daughter-in-law and a selfish wife.

The relatives and neighbors were waiting for us. I didn't know most of them. But I knew I was being watched—I was a woman from Tokyo. They probably knew why Suguru hadn't come home to live with his mother. After Suguru, I was led to his mother's bed. I apologized and asked for her forgiveness in my heart. From what I heard, she was a remarkable woman, physically weak but intelligent, beautiful and hardworking. I respected her but I hadn't had a chance to know her closely. I truly regretted that she died living alone but I couldn't cry. I couldn't shed a tear.

Suguru was busy. He went out with some relatives to make the funeral arrangements and to take care of other things. Because I didn't know any local customs, I was put in charge of the kitchen with an old woman who knew the customs about the food on special occasions. I did what I was told to do.

The first night after the funeral, for the first time here, we were alone. Only then did Suguru tell me that our priest had told him he couldn't bury his mother's bones in the grave and that he had to take his father's bones out of the grave because it wasn't his family grave.

"What?" I said. "It has been, hasn't it?"

"Yes. My grandparents are asleep there. So is my father. Now my mother is dead. I believe he thinks he can tell me anything because we had been living in Tokyo. He said my father had had a separate household from his parents and he should have been buried in his own new grave but he had had no heart to say anything to my mother because she had been struggling. I told him that if he had had no heart to tell my mother, how could he refuse her to be with her husband! I had no time to talk nonsense, I told him," Suguru said. "Then he said that he had heard that I would be coming back home and we should discuss this matter then. I think he's getting greedy."

We stayed for a month, then returned to Tokyo. Suguru had to make all kinds of connections in Tokyo so that he could open a shop and move permanently to his home in Northern Japan. I knew I'd have to move this time but I tried to delay it. After all, his mother was no longer alone. Why should we be in such a hurry? Suguru had been in Tokyo for twelve years. He couldn't just pack a bag and leave. We took two years and then moved to Northern Japan. My parents were sad to see me leave; my mother was determined to come with us and help us settle in.

Suguru decided to work for someone until he was ready to open his shop...We needed more money. Suguru's mother had had a sweater yarn shop and Suguru was in the electrical appliance sales and repair business. There were changes to be made. While Suguru had been in Tokyo, many new people had moved into the neighborhood and many big stores in the same business had opened up. Suguru knew he would face keen competition. But this was his hometown and he felt he could succeed.

After several months of working in a store, Suguru opened his shop. My mother went back to Tokyo at this time. Many old neighbors and friends knew Suguru and remembered his parents; Suguru felt comfortable and confident.

Haruo started grade school in spring. We were finally settling down.

About a year after we arrived, the priest stopped by. Suguru was out, and the priest told me to tell Suguru that he wanted to discuss the grave as soon as possible. I gave Suguru the message but he was too busy...A number of months went by and we received a letter from the priest. He wanted us to take everybody out of the grave and discuss temporary arrangements. Suguru laughed and called the priest.

"You know I just opened my business and unless it goes well, can't do anything. You just have to be patient. My parents and I have always done our best for your temple! I have many big competitors and I'm the newcomer. I first have to safely launch my business. As soon as I do it, I'll come. Please wait!" Suguru said and hung up.

Haruo became a second grader. Business seemed to be getting better and our life was on an even keel. I was content. Then one day Suguru brought some brochures on grave sites.

"My parents deserve a beautiful and peaceful resting place. I really want a nice place," Suguru said. "After all, we'll eventually be joining them. It'll become our home, too."

I nodded my head though I wasn't really enthusiastic about the grave business...I didn't want to think about it, about dying.

"I'm in no hurry; we'll take our time; we have to make a careful selection. Just in case the priest shows up, I'll show him I'm thinking about it," Suguru said.

Early in June, Mr. Kawai, Suguru's former employer in Tokyo, called. Suguru was out.

"Mrs. Asai, I want your husband to come to see us next week for a week. We're having a party for all our employees. I know you have to close your store while he is in Tokyo. But I'll make it up to you," Mr. Kawai said. "Please tell your husband that we're eagerly expecting him. I hope everything is going well for you all."

As soon as I gave Suguru the message, he called to tell Mr. Kawai he would come to Tokyo.

"I wish I could go to Tokyo!" I said. "I haven't seen my parents for..."

"But Haruo has school. Wait until Haruo's summer vacation. You two can go to see your parents," Suguru said. "Better yet, I'll bring them here!"

"Mother will come but I don't know about Father. Maybe you can persuade him. My brothers can take care of his business," I said.

Suguru loved my parents and my parents loved him as if he were their own son. I was grateful for that.

After Suguru left for Tokyo, I felt very lonely—almost like an abandoned child. It was the first time I was alone with Haruo in Northern Japan, far from my own hometown. It seemed absurd to feel so lonely because I am a grown woman, but I did. Every day I counted the days until Suguru's return. Finally the week passed but he returned without my parents.

"They'll be coming by Haruo's summer vacation," Suguru said. "We can all have a wonderful vacation together. We'll take them to Lake Towada!"

"Oh, I've always wanted to go there!" I said.

"These two kimonos are for you from the Kawais. And these three cars are for Haruo from Papa because Haruo took care of Mama while Papa was away," Suguru said.

"Thank you, Papa!" Haruo hugged the cars.

"Mr. Kawai paid for my train fare—both ways. And all other expenses. And because I closed my store for a week, he's sending me some merchandise as gifts. I was going to purchase them in Tokyo for my store," Suguru said.

"That was very generous of them. They like you. You worked hard for them," I said. "These kimonos are very expensive! I'll write them a thank-you note."

"We'll send them some fish, too," Suguru said.

He'd had a wonderful time in Tokyo, I could tell. My parents were coming soon. I was happy, too.

One morning in mid-July, Suguru went to deliver a new TV set to a customer. An hour later, I had a call and was told that Suguru's car had been hit by a huge truck and he was being taken to the hospital.

"Oh, my God! He must have been on his way home." For a few

seconds, I couldn't move. The big truck suddenly had come out of a lane, ignoring the traffic signal. Suguru was a very careful and excellent driver. "It's not fair!" I kept saying as I tried to stand up to leave for the hospital. Somehow I couldn't move as fast as I wanted to; it was as if all my strength had seeped out.

On my arrival at the hospital, I was told that Suguru had been killed almost instantly. My feet gave way and I slid to the floor. A doctor and nurse helped me up and walked me to where Suguru was lying. I heard my own voice screaming, "No! No! He can't! He can't be dead! Doctor, you can save him! You can do something! You can't just let him die! Please! You must revive him!

"Please wake up, Suguru! Please don't go!" I screamed, shaking Suguru's hand. "Haruo and I need you! How can we keep going without you?"

I cried endlessly...I didn't know what to do but first I called Haruo in school and Suguru's relatives and my parents. I was like two persons—one who was managing to do the minimum of necessary things like a robot and the other who just grieved.

Haruo was small for his age, just as Suguru had been when he was a boy. Haruo looked smaller to me now. When my parents arrived the next morning, they were a great help in just being with me. Everybody's attitudes towards me was different from what I remembered when Suguru's mother had died.

My parents quietly suggested I come back to Tokyo after everything was done here because they knew I couldn't live in Northern Japan without Suguru—Suguru's relatives and I spoke almost different languages. Haruo was too small to take over Suguru's business. I had never worked in my life. How could I survive here?

Two years ago, I'd have decided to go back but now I was different. I couldn't just leave as if Suguru's plans, Suguru's life here, our life together here had meant nothing to me. No, I couldn't' go back to Tokyo.

My parents couldn't believe my reaction. Somehow Suguru's relatives learned of my decision and were pleased. Some of them even said I was like Suguru's mother, who had won their respect soon after she married Suguru's father. It was the highest compliment and I had never imagined I would earn it.

The priest told me not to bury Suguru together with his parents. He also told me to take Suguru's parents out of the grave. I tried to argue but he kept repeating that he would keep all the bones in the temple until I found a new family grave. He mentioned an exorbitant price for keeping the bones. For the time being, I agreed. I had too many things to take care of.

"Momoko, are you sure you want to stay here? How can you manage?" My father was frantic as he prepared to go home.

"I will have to manage," I said. "Somehow."

My parents looked at each other, greatly distressed.

"Suguru wanted to take you to Lake Towada," I said. "Some day I'll take you both."

My parents again looked at each other. My father left—it was two weeks after the funeral. My mother stayed.

"Haruo is only a second grader. What are you going to do with the store?" my mother said, utterly dismayed.

"I'm trying to find someone from among Suguru's relatives who can manage it. Now that they know I'm staying, they want to help me," I said. "They've begun to like me...They were sure I'd leave but I haven't."

This was no comfort to my mother. She sighed.

"No matter what, I'm going to make it until Haruo grows up and takes over the business. I have to be strong until Haruo has a wife and many children. I'm going to keep fighting!" I said.

"Momoko, Haruo might not go into his father's business! And young brides nowadays don't want to live with a mother-in-law," my mother said. "You might have to live all alone here."

"Then it serves me right," I said. "I can't complain about it, can I? I should have lived with Suguru's mother. If I have to live alone, I'll live alone just like she did. I'm going to keep fighting until Haruo has a wife and children."

"Maybe you'll be lucky and have a nice daughter-in-law," she said, not convincingly.

"I'll have to sell some of the kimonos you made for me before my wedding, to pay to that greedy priest and to buy a grave," I said. "I never thought I'd have to sell my kimonos or have to buy a grave by myself."

"I'm glad if the kimonos can help you," Mother said. "Speaking of kimonos, Suguru's mother must have left you her kimonos!"

"Yes! I completely forgot! Oh, yes. She has many beautiful ones! She left them all to me. I didn't give her anything," I said.

"Well, you'll be buying her a new grave. I feel better now that I know you have many kimonos to sell," my mother said.

My mother left after two months, promising to come back soon.

Two months after the funeral, I paid the priest. Three months later, I had a young man for the store. Six months later, I bought a grave! I had a lot of help from Suguru's relatives and my parents, for which I'm grateful, and I slowly began to feel proud of myself. I didn't sell any kimono my mother-in-law left me. I decided to wear her kimonos. She would like that, I decided.

I also decided to learn from the relatives as much as I could about my mother-in-law because I want to gain inner strength, such as she had had; I want to have the kind of understanding she had had. She hadn't blamed Suguru or me for not coming home sooner. She'd let Suguru live his life; she'd let us live our life. I know the going will not be smooth. I'm sure to face lots of disappointments and heartaches. But I will think about my mother-in-law. She will be a superb example for me, and I hope Haruo and his wife, when he marries, will come to respect and love me as I have Suguru's mother.

Teruko Hyuga is the pseudonym of Hisako Hasegawa. Born in 1934, in Japan, she has been writing stories since her teens. She is fluent in Japanese and English, having perfected her English working at an American Army base in Japan. She now writes for children as well as for adults. Her most recent stories are written in English. She is presently in the USA.

"I can't count the number of times I have relived that awful scene in my mind: trying to make sense of it..."

L'Italiana

BY FRANCIS EBEJER

LAST year, in Italy...

I used to be awakened, I could swear, by the same sea gull. Round about seven. I don't think it missed out once during the whole week I was a houseguest there. Normally I'm pretty good at not letting curiosity get the better of me. But when on the last morning of my stay I heard the sea gull's cry again, I promptly got out of bed and went to look out of the window.

About a quarter of a kilometer farther down from the southernmost gardens of the villa, and a sling-shot away from the main church of Bellagio, the waters of Lago di Como were like a vast, dull glaze in the first rays of an insipid sun. I looked down at the terrace below and, sure enough, there it was, as large as life, perched on top of a stone urn at one corner of the balustrated ledge, head inclined to one side, one steady eye fixed on my face, and calling: eeeegh, eeegh...

It used to embarrass me to find Margherita already waiting for me for breakfast.

I'm usually punctual, though nothing like her. I always knew her to be scrupulously on time, invariably; always ahead of me, practically in everything.

In the matter of intuition, for instance. She had this unique knack of seeing straight into things, right from the word go! I can't remember her ever failing once. While I? Still far behind, and so slow, just as if I were congenitally incapable of ever seeing farther than my nose.

As she always did, she again bade me sit on her left. Always on her left! She had a scar on the right side of her face and I wasn't supposed to gaze at it too much. I'd often tried to reassure her that it didn't bother me. She carried on thinking it did.

Some years after her injury she had allowed herself to submit to cosmetic surgery. The operation hadn't been a complete success. She had been glad. She had wanted the scar to show, not much, just a little, she told me: she had become used to it, got to like it, grown fond of it. Years passed before I could finally make out what she was trying to tell me. But then, as I said, I was pretty slow in certain, well, *deeper* things—like motives, reasons, idiosyncracies, those genuine and those contrived.

I told her about the sea gull and she smiled.

"D'you know what I think it is, Sander?" she said with a mischievous voice and glance. "The unquiet soul of somebody you might have once turned your back on, culpably or not, and now it just won't leave you in peace. *Ecco!*"

Old friends that we were, we liked pulling each other's leg. And that morning last year, that morning of the alarm-clock sea gull, surely, that's exactly what she was doing. Pulling my leg again!

I said to myself: It's conscience which won't let you rest, not some wandering soul, not some stupid ghost.

But I said nothing of that, nothing that would have given her the reply I thought she deserved, for she had begun to laugh. And I laughed with her. And I ate well that morning.

I still find it difficult to believe that a half-century (46 years to be exact) has passed since I first set eyes on her.

Forty-six years ago, and if it seems like yesterday, that's because it's true: life, existence, isn't that just one moment of cosmic time, they tell us?

One of the fiercest air raids had just come to an end. A stunned and uncanny stillness now hung over the whole of Malta. I had counted no fewer than eighteen Junkers 88, thirteen Heinkels and an almost equal number of Stukas, all escorted by swarms of Messerschmitts. On the *All Clear* signal, I did what I always used to do: ran out of the village as fast as my legs could carry me and straight on to the top of the southern cliffs at Gebel Ciantar, with Verdala Castle and Buskett Gardens opposite on one side, and my village, Dingli, on the other; behind me and far below, the Mediterranean.

From that spot, I could better view the dense smoke rising and completely obscuring the sky above Valletta, the Three Cities and Hal Fav and Luqa airdromes. Watching the devastation, and sorrowing, I picked wild dwarf figs and ate them as if each mouthful were a feast in itself, and my stomach growled unstoppably for more. I was tall for my age, and thin and hungry.

Then I saw her. Sitting, knees drawn up, in a sun deceitfully peaceful and radiant. Far behind her, Filfla Rock stood above the sea's surface like a tombstone on the grave of a civilization that had once thought there was nothing like it under the sun...

Just the two of us in that expanse of rock and shrub. The minute she became aware of me, she waved, an impulsive gesture, and didn't stop waving until she saw me move. Clumsy and on legs suddenly gone unreliable, completely gauche, I made my way towards her over jagged fissures in the rock. We stood regarding each other for a few seconds, then I held out three figs to her. We munched away, crunching the tiny seeds in near-comic unison.

The way she uttered *grazie* immediately stamped her to my ears as Italian. Strange. An Italian citizen in a British colony, at that precise moment locked in battle, no holds barred, with Mussolini's Italy?

After the initial hesitancy, we began to converse in earnest. She, in refined, inflected Italian, with me desperately trying to remember some of the Italian I had learned at the Lyceum: bits and pieces of

Manzoni and Leopardi and Torquato Tasso. However, my mind soon turned to spies. I begged her to get off that rock. "And why?" she wanted to know. I stuttered something feeble about my fear that soldiers might see her, discover she was Italian, an enemy alien, and...

She at last gave a chuckle, slithered down and settled, knees up again, near a patch of marjoram. I was fifteen; she looked my age. We couldn't stop talking. I didn't pick any more figs that day...

Her face looked fairer than I had imagined at a distance; auburn, marcelled hair in slight disarray; sensitive eyes the color of Mediterranean rock, brown with shades of orange.

"So how is it you're in Malta?"

"Just because I'm Italian?" She smiled teasingly at me.

To hide the fact that I had no ready reply to give her, I cast my glance on a flight of sea gulls scouting individually along the precipice below us, then, as if at some instinctive, tribal signal, all together veering off over the Mediterranean and as far as the eyes could see.

I had the odd impression then, I remember, that they wanted to be as far away from us as possible. Their flight seemed to convey a kind of reprimand to us human beings for the destruction our vaunted intelligence had managed to bring down on the world, which happened to belong to them, too. It was as if the blood that was being shed just because people like us two were of different nationalities was something entirely alien to their comprehension and to their dignity—and their common sense.

A farm-dog barked suddenly from the roof of a farmhouse in the valley.

My Italian became more fluent and I could understand hers better. Soon we were talking as if we had known each other for years, so much so that she was soon telling me about her family.

Yes, her father, the Marquis, was at that moment a high-ranking officer in Mussolini's Army. And her mother? Serving in a military hospital outside Lecce. At least, that's what she had been given to understand.

"And you yourself? An Italian...Italian passport..."

"English."

"Your parents Italian and you...*English?*"

"We had already been living on this Island four years before the war broke out," she began irrelevantly. "My father often used to travel to Italy; I don't know what he was doing. *É un tipo piuttosto introverso.* We had become great friends of a British military family here...My parents left for Italy when the situation started getting worse in 1939. I hope you are understanding what I'm saying, are you?"

Not really. A single thought had put me off balance.

"And they left you behind!"

I was also easily surprised in those days. And then, too, there's no holding youngsters from passing judgment on their elders at the slightest opportunity...On the other hand, isn't that perhaps what youngsters are for: as a permanent and visible warning to their elders not to allow their past idealism to be sacrificed on the altar of materialistic expediency? But never mind that. I had really got hot under the collar, and I must have shown it for she smiled and her smile remained on her face for a long time. (Now, yes, now I know what else was behind that smile of forty-six years ago; and it wasn't just amusement at my anger).

"We are a very old Tuscan family," she began explaining patiently. "If there are any relatives left, then we don't know of them, but I doubt it. The family's had its day! My parents knew they would be living and working apart from each other, and I would have been left on my own...This English family...well, he, a Brigadier in the First Dorset Regiment...he and his wife and three children sort of adopted me: they have pleasant memories of Italy before the War. This is a British colony and they knew how to go about getting me to stay on in Malta without hindrance and not too conspicuously; so they made me English, like them. We live in an eighteenth century house between Siggiewi and Girgenti. Do you know which one I mean? I love coming up here..."

I think the best Italian that I came out with was when I said: "So, you here, they in Italy. And from Italy they're sending us nothing but bombs and Germans."

Her smile disappeared and her face grew serious. "Who knows where's the best place to be?" She lowered her head. "In the grave perhaps?" she added in a low voice.

But that must have been just a brief second's mood for she soon raised her eyes again (pretending?) to follow the flight of a bird above us. I could just see some tears in her eyes (that wasn't surprising: the sun was strong and, in the sun, one's eyes tend to water, don't they?...At least, that's how it looked to me just then).

"A chaffinch," she exclaimed, happy to have recognized it.

The least I could do, I felt, was to agree. "Yes, a chaffinch." (A goldfinch, more likely).

After that, there was no more mention of her parents.

Now and then we met and walked along the cliffs. Once I took her to my home. More visits followed.

My mother and sisters took to her at once. My elder sister was soon taking a hand. I told her where to get off. In those days the star in my romantic firmament was another— "Curly Top" Pawlina in the house with the green shutters near the horse-trough.

Soon after the War the *Marchesa* turned up in Malta again, this time to take Margherita back with her to Italy. As for the Marquis, apparently it hadn't taken him long to realize that his once beautiful dream of a new Italy had turned into rank betrayal of his country: he had joined the partisans of Reggio Emilia, been captured by the retreating Germans and executed by them.

The years passed. In the 1950s, she invited me to their villa on Lake Como. That time I had gone for two weeks. We continued to write to each other after that, more she than I, as my life had veered to other spheres and been overtaken by other commitments. She invited me again several times but the right opportunity never seemed to arise for me.

In the early Sixties, I began receiving her letters from England where she had gone to live after marrying one of the Brigadier's nephews. They spent some time in Singapore. On being widowed, she returned to Bellagio and her villa there. Today, her son is an executive at the Fiat plant in Russia; her daughter will be getting married next year to an Argentinian cultural delegate at the United Nations headquarters in New York.

The last time I saw her, as I said, was last year, when I spent that week at her villa on my way to Bolzano: the week of the inspired sea gull. She had already phoned me several times—we had never before spoken "long distance"—before I finally made up my mind to go and see her. There might have been some urgency which I didn't notice then, and which I'm only now acknowledging, in retrospect. Not once did it cross my mind that she might have been in poor health, either during that week's visit or at any time during the last few months.

Yesterday, Monday, I received news of her death. She died last Thursday.

But I haven't said everything yet. Her scar. What had happened was this.

During the War, I had the habit of carrying a Swiss knife with me. I was never without it (poor Uncle Salv spent practically the entire War looking for it). With the main blade out, nine inches all told. For prickly pears, bunches of grapes, cabbages, peaches, potatoes, honeycombs in the rock or the odd tin of preserved food from a negligently guarded Officers' Mess.

Why not, too, as a defense weapon against some Nazi or other who might have carelessly taken it into his head to pounce on me from behind a rubble-wall or from inside a cave in the cliffs? There's no saying where a youngster's imagination might not lead him, especially if he were hungry, as I was, almost all the time...

One afternoon I was walking her back to her home after a couple of hours on the cliffs together when we heard the Siggiewi air-raid siren. We barely gave it any notice, we just went on walking. We only stopped to look up at the overweening Luftwaffe passing directly overhead on its way to Grand Harbour and the airdromes. We had stopped below a wall-niche of St. Nicholas, and it was there, in all that noise and confusion, that I was suddenly gripped by the weirdest bout of madness I had ever experienced.

Wrenching the Swiss knife from my pocket, I flicked the blade out, raised it above my head and started to jump and yell and slash the air just as I used to watch the Red Indians doing in cowboy films. It had all started as an inane bit of clowning, but, soon enough, I wasn't seeing Indians and cowboys anymore but a long, ghoulish procession of my country's enemies throughout its centuries. I don't know how many of Hitler's air squadrons I destroyed in those few minutes!

Then, suddenly...blood, real blood, on my hands, in my eyes. I had hit her in the face. All my senses seemed to abandon me; I cowered and believe I wept, while nothing, not a sound from her, except "Nothing...nothing..." And obscene sounds in the sky and, far off yet rocking the earth under us, the thud of bombs, until that and the insane hammering inside my head became indistinguishable one from the other.

A couple of farming families took us in and, after sending for a doctor, saw to her wound, cleaned us as best they could, and gave us drink.

I can't count the number of times I have relived that awful scene in my mind: trying to make sense of it, exorcise myself of its haunting. The picture would blur; when just about to narrow into focus, it would blur again.

While I was fooling about with the knife, she had gone to stand a good ten paces away from me in the shelter of a garden wall and next to a ficus tree, one of her elbows (a vivid memory this) just touching a bucket on the rim of a well.

If so, how then could I have struck her from where I was? And with the knife still in my hands?

It was only yesterday, soon after I had heard of her death, that the true picture suddenly cleared for me; the scales, as they say, fell from my eyes.

There was no doubt about it. She herself had run up to me...had known exactly what she was doing, had actually, deliberately, run up to the knife. And made contact. Now, today, I'm ready to swear to that, even though everything had happened in that negligible second it had taken my knife to come down on her face.

What had she tried to convey with her action?

Or—this comes to me now—was it after all her way of expiating with some of her blood the faults of others?

Yes, but whose? Her mother's and father's? Fascist Italy's? Nazi Germany's? Colonial Britain's? Those of a humanity that had lost

Its head? Of a decadent civilization with its so-called values? *Mine?* But what was I other than blind, and hopelessly stupid?

She wanted the scar to show, she had told me. She wanted it to show, even if just a little, she had told me, smiling, several times.

Memento Mori.

I'll have prayers said for her. But I'm far from sure who needs them more—she, or I?

How is the sin of insensitivity expiated and forgiven and, with luck, forgotten?

Where I live in Malta, no sea gulls ever fly.

This morning, however, early, I woke up to the cry of one. I went to look out of the window. Nothing but inscrutable sky.

One thing I know for certain—and no one will gainsay me—tomorrow I will hear it again. And the morning after. And the morning after that...

And at dawn on each of any other days left to me.

Born and raised in Malta, Francis Ebejer is a successful short story writer, novelist and playwright whose work appears in Malta, England and the USA. His early plays are credited with starting the modern theater in Malta. A bilingual writer (English and Maltese) he also writes and produces television plays.

"It was deathly silent everywhere."

A Clear Day in May

BY JOHAN BORGEN

THE whole city was waiting for the eclipse. The whole city was talking about the eclipse. Old Bino stepped out of his shanty that stood by itself out on the open plain. He sniffed the air and asked, "Will it come soon?"

"What?" a young man's voice was close to his ear. "What are you talking about, Old Man?"

"What am I talking about?—The eclipse, of course! Will it come soon?"

The young man's laughter blended with a young woman's giggle.

"We don't know anything about any eclipse," she chuckled light-heartedly. "Anyway, Old Bino, it'll be all the same to you. You won't see any difference." They were young and in love.

"How do you happen to know me?" Old Bino tried to initiate a conversation and to create a picture of them behind his blind eyes.

"Everybody loves Old Bino." The young woman wanted to make him feel good. "Look here, Bino," she blurted out in her youthful nonchalant way. "We've brought you a fried chicken and a bottle of currant wine. Mother made the wine herself year before last, and

84

it has just been tapped on a clear day in May."

"A clear day in May," Bino echoed pensively. "I thank the young lady and gentleman for this generous gift."

They snickered. All young people were amused when Old Bino attempted to be formal. They watched him and pitied him. A putrid stench came out of that black hole, the entrance to the shanty. But somehow Bino himself seemed clean, almost like a child. Behind his blind eyes there was a keen brain. The whole city was aware of that. People said that at one time this aging half-wit had been a man of great potential, moreover a happy and perceptive person with genuine appreciation of everything beautiful in life.

He set the gifts carefully on the ground beside his shanty, near the black hole where there was shade.

"A clear day in May," he mumbled again. "Yes, just like today."

"Just like today," the young man repeated, only for the sake of saying something. And, "Exactly," remarked the young woman, also only to be saying something. "But what's that about an eclipse that Bino talks about?"

"Really, don't you know?" Old Bino's question had a hint of irritation. "Don't you know that a total eclipse is on the way, and it'll come under the most opportune circumstances at the precise moment—at 12:10, and it'll last ten minutes—that's how long there will be a total eclipse. Well," he added more softly, "people have to be young and in love not to know about the eclipse that everybody's talking about."

"Well, that's what we are!" the young woman smiled. The young man cleared his throat and asked, "Why do you say the most opportune circumstances?"

"Because it's naturally most exciting when the sun is at its highest!" Old Bino was emphatic. "If it had been at midnight or at some time in the afternoon or, for instance, in January, or had the day been cloudy, or had it occurred in an entirely different area—! Can't you see how wonderfully everything concurs?"

"Yes!" The young man looked at his watch. "Then it's not more than twenty minutes from now. Where do you think we'd have the best view, Bino?"

Bino nodded knowingly. "Twenty minutes. Then we have just enough time to get there."

Nimble as a cat he had stooped down and set the gifts inside the shanty. When he bobbed up again, he had a basket on his arm.

"Come," he urged. "We'll go to the City Square. That's where everybody'll be."

Agile and sure-footed he walked on uneven ground, carrying his basket carefully.

"What do you have in your basket, Bino?" asked the young man close enough to speak to him. "Yes, what do you have in your basket?" repeated the young woman. She was so madly in love that the very sound of the young man's voice was ecstatic to her, so ecstatic that his question had to be repeated. And he was so much in love that the echo of his own question from her lips was like music of words replete with the most profound meaning.

"See for yourself." Bino did not slacken his pace but drew aside the paper covering the basket.

"Pieces of black glass!" The young man was puzzled.

"I'll sell those on the City Square. People are so scatterbrained. There'll be many who have forgotten their dark glasses, and those who have them—well, even very dark glasses are not enough when it's a matter of looking directly at the sun. That's why I've been busy for many days cutting bits of glass and smoking them so people can look at the eclipse without going blind."

"How much do you charge for such a piece of smoked glass?" The young man was curious.

"That varies according to what people can afford. The wealthiest are the hardest to please. But then, too, they're always the most worried about their eyes."

The young people exchanged glances. Old Bino's experiences always made a point.

"But the two of you will each get a piece of glass from me, and that will be gratis."

"No, no," the young man protested when they were given the bits of glass. "We didn't bring those little gifts with the idea that you should give us gifts in return." He took money from his pocket and tried to put it into Bino's hand. The Old Man pushed his hand away.

"Nor is that the reason I want to give you something," Bino said as he walked faster. The young woman had to run to keep up.

"Why is it then?" she asked.

"Because you're so deeply in love."

Again the young people looked at one another. The young man dropped the coins back into his pocket. He felt suddenly moved. The young woman also was silent and emotional. She tested the smoked glass against the sky. It really was getting very dark. All at once she was frightened.

When they reached the City Square, it was crammed with people. There was not space enough even for a squirrel on the State House steps...It was a small State House, extremely small, in fact, too old and unfit for use, and therefore the pride of the city. And if it did not lend itself to anything else, it was superbly situated for viewing the eclipse at midday because it faced directly south.

All other steps and stairs at the Square were also swarming with people, and the Square itself crowded with onlookers. Little children had been lifted up high on the shoulders of adults. Bigger ones had climbed up on everything that could be climbed onto. The bronze fountain in the center—it was bronze, in the shape of swans, herons, and other wild creatures with necks stretching in all directions—it was like a big shrub alive with living fruit. In the lindens and the chestnut trees bordering the Square on all sides, birds with upturned throats were singing among fresh green leaves. Many children had horns and whistles. They blew them incessantly. And those who had none to blow just made noise and laughed loudly. Blinds came down in front of most shops. Owners and workers streamed out and chimed in with the rest of the noise-makers. There was racket and clanging enough to stop age-old bells from ringing and clocks from striking.

But they did not. Suddenly they joined in with their own heavy clanging and thumping. At first it got quiet as on a solemn holiday, but shortly astounding commotion broke out again.

The two young people and Bino had arrived at their destination in good time before the clocks began to strike twelve. They pushed their way forward among people who called to them and greeted them. Their love affair was commonly known in the little city. People rejoiced with them. They were handsome and happy. Old Bino was somewhere between a popular eccentric and a tolerated disgrace in the town with his miserable and not totally alcohol-free life in his shanty on the plain. But today he was welcomed along with the other unusual manifestations. And when he uncovered the very practical contents of his basket, from the very first moment sales went as swift as lightning. Many had already suffered bitter consequences of stealthy glances at the day's topic of conversation.

At first, however, the sun showed no signs of darkening. Bino, completely confused in sense of direction amid the jostling crowd, worked his way forward. "Here, Bino!—Here!" mischievous children teased and yelled. That caused him to bump directly into the most venerable citizens or to rush blindly at the fountain. No one saw anything tragic about Bino. His sharp tongue and dissolute life had put him beyond conventional sympathy. Finally someone got him placed on the edge of the fountain, and there he sat with his empty basket in his lap, staring expectantly into his own private darkness.

In spite of the hubbub the young people had found a spot on the bottom step of the State House stairs, where they were welcomed with laughter and cheers and quickly became part of the noisy throng. Twelve melancholy strokes of the State House clock sounded across the City Square, horns blared, a silver bell chimed from a high balcony. A big woman at an open window stopped eating. She found the whole spectacle disgusting and let people know it.

In a surprisingly strong voice Bino announced, "Now the eclipse is beginning!" Those nearby heard him. "The eclipse!" they whispered. "The eclipse! The eclipse!"

Immediately the noise subsided. One group after another became quiet. Still there was the echo of the last stroke of the clock. Still the echo hung in the air. People started to look up toward the sun, but it continued to shine down on them from its place in the heavens with no discernible sign of darkening.

"How do you know that?" asked those nearest to Bino.

"The birds! They have stopped singing!"

People listened. They all listened. The birds in the linden trees around the City Square had actually stopped singing. It was deathly silent everywhere.

The young woman whispered to the young man. "He heard the eclipse starting." She had turned pale under her light sunburn.

Now they saw it. At first it was like the coming of a dark fog, not only over the sun but over everything in the air. They could not really see it, but it was there—like a defect in vision.

The young woman clung to her lover's arm. "Is this the eclipse?" she whispered.

"Wait." He spoke softly and clasped her hand. It was cold. "Are you freezing?" For an instant he took the dark glass from before his eyes.

"I'm frightened," she replied. But he did not hear her. She looked around at the people. She did not look up toward the sun. She saw the people getting smaller and their faces turning darker. She saw the leaves changing to dark green and folding together on their stems. She watched the reflection of the arched windows of the church fade from gold to lead. Step by step the world was losing its luster, its life. There was still light, but it was as if a shadow of death was covering all that had glittered. And she felt a veil within herself. What had sparkled in her spirit now sparkled no more. Darkness would assail her from without and meet a darkness deep within that she had forgotten could be lurking there. Deep inside her there was a cry without sound because there was no one to hear it.

Abruptly it became darker. A sigh went through the crowd. Most of the people discarded their pieces of dark glass and stared fearlessly directly at the sun. It was getting smaller and smaller. It was no longer only the surroundings that were dim. The sun itself disappeared from sight. People stood speechless, knowing the heavenly bodies were moving and noting that they themselves were a moving part of the universe, that they were in the space and a part of this space and that they and this space were equally powerless in their fellowship. A cold distrust went from person to person without their seeing one another, all knowing that no one could help anyone, not with anything in any way.

Night settled over the City Square and over the city, over all that they knew and comprehended to be The Earth. Some began to lower their bits of glass from their eyes and look around, and they were shocked to discover it was almost as black around them as it had been while they looked upward through smoked glass. Neighbors with whom they had everyday acquaintance had taken on strange facial expressions. Necks they had seen year out and year in looked at once to be old necks. Happy, cheerful faces that had inspired confidence and mirth just by chance meetings on the City Square had taken on a languid appearance with alien and hopeless aspects.

The young woman held onto the young man's arm in an attempt to draw him away with her. But he was concerned only with what was happening in the sky. He had tossed away the smoked glass by now and with open eyes looked upward at the mystery and could not tear himself away.

But to her came words, unfamiliar words whose meanings she had never probed to their depth. War. Destruction. Ruin. Annihilation. Nothingness. Words that had signified this and that to her, nothing much, just sounds and letters. Now they came before her and within her with a new and different meaning that changed both what she saw and what she thought—and yet it was as if they conjured up something she once had pondered or felt but had since forgotten. Slowly and reluctantly she freed herself from the young man's arm and looked curiously at her own hand and arm and at the arm she had freed herself from and then down on her own person and up toward him who was staring upward and all around. She noticed his mouth was slightly open as if he were asleep or overcome by the mystery of obliteration without realizing what it was that absorbed him.

The weather turned cold. People felt it and half absent-mindedly put on coats and shawls. A little child cried from an open window. Immediately more children began to cry. Parents leaned over them with clumsy explanations. The baker's well-fed St. Bernard tried to make himself sleek and thin and crept from the fountain directly across the City Square and scratched at the door of the bakeshop, whimpering painfully. But it was locked, and the blinds rolled down to keep out the sun.

Bino did not look up. He sat on the edge of the fountain, staring out blindly. He heard the sounds around him, and he felt the silence. He was aware of the cold creeping in over the Square and in among the people. He knew from the general movement of the crowd what they were experiencing and how frightened they were. Yes, now in the darkness they were almost on common footing.

But he did not share their apprehension for he was acquainted with emptiness through an entire lifetime of night.

"Do you see it's getting lighter!" said the young man confidently to the young woman. He spoke as if it were his personal accomplishment.

But she was not there. Now he first noticed that she was not holding onto his arm, that she had not done so for some time. How long? He looked around helplessly. "Where are you?" he shouted. But his question was drowned by the babble of surrounding voices. "It's getting lighter! It's getting lighter!" Where are you?"

"It's lighter!" everyone cried out at once. "Lighter!"

Still darkness was filling the atmosphere, but then like the wing of a powerful bird moving across the sky above them, the fog also dispersed and gave way to beams of light. At first it seemed to come in small specks. Then light engulfed them. People celebrated and laughed, at first somewhat shyly. They would be embarrassed to have anyone know they had been terrorized. Again they brought out their bits of smoked glass and all faces turned upward in cheerful confidence, perhaps a little forced.

Presently the birds began to twitter, cautiously at first as if testing from branch to branch. Then all at once there was an exultant chorus in all the trees around the Square. Children had stopped crying. The baker's St. Bernard recovered his natural coat and lifted his head. He sat in the sunshine in front of the shop, relieving himself and dirtying the sidewalk.

All were uncommonly merry as if they had drunk wine. Since children could not reach heights alone, adults lifted them and shouted, "The sun!" The children rubbed their eyes against the light and laughed at the adults who were acting as if the sun were something extraordinary. The noise of excitement resounded from stairways, shops, and trees. A young man had climbed to the top of the fountain in the center of the City Square to a most amazing position among the necks of the bronze creatures. He threw his hat into the air and yelled, "Hurrah for the sun!"

Shops and taverns opened. People flocked in to buy food and drinks, each according to his preference. The big woman slammed her window shut again and resumed eating. She had stopped for awhile. She said only, "Is that all there is?"

The young man elbowed his way forward between people along the walls of buildings, shoving aside the slender ones, circumventing the broader ones, bumping into many, and talking the whole time.

"Where are you?" he called constantly. He was driven to desperation. He began to feel guilty, to fear he had deserted her.

People were leaving the center of the Square, drifting toward the outer limits and onto the streets. Only a few still remained near the fountain. Soon they, too, went away, and then he caught sight of her.

At the edge of the fountain sat Old Bino with his basket. She was standing in front of him, face to face, her eyes fixed on the blind man.

The young man raced across the Square. Breathless and worried, he took her into his arms. But she was limp in his embrace, cold, pale, and unresponsive. "I have been so anxious about you."

She did not look up but kept her head bent low as if expecting a blow.

"Are you still afraid?"

"Yes," she whispered so quietly that he could barely hear her.

"But now the sun has come back!" he assured her.

She did not answer. He followed the direction of her eyes toward the old man.

"Now I understand," he said to comfort her. "You are thinking about him, that this is the way it always is for him—that it must be dreadful."

She still did not look up. "It isn't that."

"Isn't it?" he asked thoughtfully. He was standing there with the young woman he loved. A short while ago they had run across the open field together. They had not even known there would be an eclipse. They had not been aware of anything. They had been happy. Now they were alone on the City Square. They stood close to one another, but he could not reach her.

"Shall we help you home, Old Man?" The young man spoke to Bino just to get something off his mind, but his eyes were on her. He was accustomed to her repeating questions that he asked, but this time she did not.

Old Bino stood up, shook his head, and walked away mumbling. He moved slowly with steady steps and in the right direction.

"What did he mean by that? 'A clear day in May'?" The young man wondered. "Oh, now I know. He remembered about the wine!"

He looked at her lovingly and held her close to him. He was afraid she might fall.

"Bino saw it," she remarked. He looked at her mouth, wanting to draw out her meaning.

"What did Old Bino see? Dearest, what is it?" he urged.

He lifted her head to force an answer or to enable him to read it in her face. He wanted something to happen, something to be said. "What is it, Darling? Tell me."

She did not look into his eyes. "Nothing," she whispered. "Only everything."

Johan Borgen holds a place among Norway's most important authors of this century. A satirist, moralist, non-conformist, sensitive literary artist, he has written in every genre but excels in the short story and novel. He was educated at the University of Oslo. From 1928 to 1941 he was a full-time columnist for Dagbladet, *Oslo's leading newspaper. He has published more than 40 books, served 6 years as editor of* Vindeut *(literary magazine), and has worked as a stage director and radio commentator. He was confined to prison camp during the Nazi Occupation; later he joined the Resistance Movement and was forced to flee to Sweden. In 1965 Mr. Borgen was awarded an annual literary prize by Norway's national government. In 1972 he was a second-time winner of the national short story contest. His gifted translator is the gracious and dependable Amanda Langemo who grew up in a bilingual home in the Norwegian-American community of Kenyon, Minnesota. Amanda Langemo teaches at the university level, is a book reviewer and freelance writer.*

"There's always a reason."

The Exile

BY F. SIONIL JOSÉ

IT was a recurrent dream and it was not pleasant because when it was over and he was once more awake, his mouth was always dry and there was this wild tightening in his chest that seemed to squeeze all breath away. He had never found out what caused it although he had developed some theories about it. Perhaps, it was the heavy lunch that did it—the codfish fried in olive oil, the grapes and the bottle of muscatel. He took a nap and then it happened—he was sinking once more in a bottomless pool and flailing his arms, his lungs close to bursting. He had never learned how to swim and this fact—even in a silly thing like a dream—was real and chilling. But always, in that very moment when it seemed as if he was about to die or his lungs would burst, salvation came, and he was being towed up to the light. Once it was his mother who did this and once it was Nena. But in most cases he woke up clutching the sheets, sweating or—as Nena once told him during this nightmare—screaming.

He had not experienced the dream for a long time and the fact that it happened again oppressed him and impinged upon him the fact that one cannot really run away from oneself and that the only sure escape is in that dreamless sleep from which there is no waking.

He turned around to the familiar dimensions of his room aglow with the mellow light of a June afternoon and he was at once assured that he was, indeed, in this small Basque hotel, thousands of miles away from the merciless ravage of home and that in this room, they were all in their places: the porcelain washbowl, the old pine cabinet which sagged to the floor, his battered suitcase and his easel. He sighed; his breathing slowly resumed its rhythm and when his senses were sharp and clear again, he smelled the pine and the wax and the sharp odor of the cheese that was on the table beside his bed. Yes, he was in this small Basque hotel and the room itself evoked all the lures that he sought, squid and merluza, grapes and wine and an appetite for all these as if they provided life's only compulsions.

In the last two weeks, his vacation in Marquina had done wonders not only for his troubled mind but also for his skin. The dark rims of oil in his fingernails which he got when he worked in that machineshop in Frankfurt had vanished. He was regaining his deftness with the pencil and the brush and, most of all, he was beginning to enjoy painting again.

The sensation of well-being quickly returned as he sat up. Beyond the window which opened to a small balcony and the plaza, a brass band was playing a waltz. He stood up and went to the window: all of Marquina was in the plaza, strolling, sitting on the stone benches or dancing in the fronton. He could go down as Elena, the maid, had suggested and join the dancing. He already had several acquaintances in the village and all were eager to entertain him but he had demurred and stayed in his room when he was not out sketching or walking in the fields and hills.

He saw the big Ford then—black, glossy and fat—drive into the village. American cars are not common in Spain, least of all in the Basque where the roads, though asphalted, are narrow and tortuous. The car stopped with a pompous screech below the hotel marquee. It was not just an American car; it carried an old Manila plate too.

Forgotten were the Basque's transient pleasures. The old anxiety rushed back and he must once more be aware of his name and progeny, for whoever owned the car was certainly coming to see him. He regretted that when he arrived he had not registered as a Thai or Mexican but as a Filipino, though not as a Reyes. There was no avoiding it, for Marquina was small, but in other places he had given different names; he was Diem, a Vietnamese, Inche Yosuf, a Malayan, or even Nakamura, a Japanese businessman. The masquerade had been successful, for he was an Asian prototype and could pass for a Korean, a Chinese or, as it happened once in the United States when he was going to New Mexico, a Hopi Indian.

He slipped on his shoes and tweed jacket, then waited for the rap on the door. When it came, he stood up and opened it to Elena, buxom and amiable, her rough, red hands gesturing, and this athletic-looking Spaniard, in his late twenties like himself. This was the first thing he noticed about Arrastequi—his athletic build. He was not muscular but there was a tautness in his features which indicated a strength held in reserve. They shook hands. "*Comusta kayo,*" the Spaniard grinned then switched back to English from the Philippine language which he spoke with a deep nasal tone.

"Please sit down," Pepe said. "I was just getting ready to go out." The call should be brief but Arrastequi apparently didn't want it that way.

"If you want to go out," he said warmly, "remember I have a car and I can take you wherever you please. Bilbao, San Sebastian—any place in the Basque. Have you seen my car?" He didn't wait for a reply, "It's a Ford and I got it in Manila. I lived there for two years, you know."

Pepe nodded.

"That car tells the story of my love," the Spaniard said. "It was a gift. I was playing at the fronton—you call it Jai Alia." He slapped his thigh in a gesture of supreme pleasure. "What a city, what a people, what hospitality!"

The Spaniard gushed and did not mind the sullenness of his listener. "Do you play Jai Alai?"

"Not really," Pepe said. "But I've been to the Skyroom—dinners and a little nightclubbing. There's a good orchestra there…"

After a few more reminiscences about Manila and his mistress,

Arrastequi stood up. They were of equal height but that was their only similarity. This was a sensuous man, given to the pleasures of the flesh, and Pepe felt repelled by him. Yet, there was something fascinating about him, his Filipina mistress for instance, and Pepe wanted to know more about her, to learn who this fool of a woman was, who fell for a loud-mouthed pelotari.

There was the morrow and Arrastequi had gotten his word that they would go out, drive to Cenaruzza, the birthplace of Simon Bolivar, then on to Guernica, the ancient capital of the Basque nation. Arrastequi said he had a debt to pay: "I like the Philippines very, very much," he repeated with great feeling. "There's no country like it. Your memories of a country, the way you feel about it are often the result of your personal relationships with its people. I cannot thank all of the Filipinos I met by being good to you. And my woman—ah! Your country is blessed. But look at Spain...most of it is rock and desert. And what grows on it? But the Philippines—there's a country!"

Again, all the angers that had long lain repressed in him were uncoiled as if some magic button which released them had been pressed right in this room, in this anonymous village beyond the reach of filial ties and the embrace of a love that was dead. And yet, he was not really freeing an old emotion; he was giving it form, articulating it. "I hate my country and people," he cried and was surprised at his vehemence, at the sudden flame that singed his face as if to warn him that what he had said was treason. But he reassured himself that he was speaking the truth: "My country is headed for the dogs and that's why I am here—away from all the mess. You ask, why shouldn't I be there pitching and being a patriot? All that mush? I once thought of staying on and fighting back, but it is hopeless. I don't fight hopeless battles. I fight for those causes which have at least a chance for survival."

"You are too harsh with your people," Arrastequi said. He had been taken aback by Pepe's truculence. "You forget I lived there for two years and what did I find? Wonderful friends—yes. And this woman. What she can do with her tongue...but let us not talk *bastos*. All I say is the Philippines is a very rich country, the people are wonderful. And if the people are also kind..."

"Kind? Kind?" Pepe checked himself for he had raised his voice again. "They are not kind. They are scum, they are greedy and indecent. They are to be butchered. Yes—and their carcasses should be stripped slowly, tendon by tendon, by vultures..."

"Surely, some of the leaders are good. Magsaysay and you know..."

"Vultures. All of them," Pepe wailed. "I want to forget them all. Listen, do you know why I am here? And do you know how I spent my time? Back home I used to go to the movies every day. Cowboy pictures. Tagalog pictures. Second-run movies. All of them. I'd sit them out. Sometimes, I was the first to go into the movie houses. And after the movies, the nightclubs. I didn't do anything. Just listened to the music. All sorts of music...and in my apartment..."

"You wasted a lot of time."

Pepe smiled. "Think so? It was better that way. It kept my mind off the mess. The dirt in the streets. When I am in a nightclub and it's dark and there's this girl singing, I am in another world. But then, I must walk out. And that's not good."

"Yes," after some reflection; "Manila is really dirty. But after a while, you don't notice the dirt any more. And you can't escape it; it has become a part of the city."

"That's it," Pepe said, the joy of confirmation racing through him. "I was afraid of that. I had started to stop caring. Do you know what that meant?"

Arrastequi shook his head.

Pepe said, "When a man stops caring, he ceases being involved, he is dead. That was what I was afraid of. I didn't want to die..."

"You really believe that?" Arrastequi asked. "No man stops caring as long as he breathes. As long as he has a mind and a memory, he will care. This is what separates us from the animals, no? We have feelings. Maybe, you don't realize this."

That night, Pepe continued to be badgered not by what he had done but at himself for having permitted his emotions to be expressed once more when he had long relinquished that luxury. But it was not only this which now riled him. Arrastequi's words had sunk into his consciousness: "You speak as if you have never loved." The Spaniard had spoken frankly and now, he mulled over the possibility that Arrastequi could be right, that he had not really known or savored the true essence of life itself. What was it—what was the real reason he had left Manila? Was it because of his father? How much simpler it would have been if his father had rejected him and told him that he was worthless and not even fit to manage a sari-sari store, which was, alas, very true. But Senator Reyes had some notions about the independence of children and he had pampered him, given him all the rope with which to hang himself and this rope was of spun gold. Yes, his father gave him certitude and the providence that wealth could assure. Was it just plain cussedness then, or boredom? But that was not so because he could have been busy if he had so preferred.

Maybe Nena—if she were still alive...maybe, she could explain. I left, perhaps, because of myself, because I wanted to be sure that I could stand alone, because I wanted to reach out to life's very depths, touch its infinite limits. This is what I want and I could have done it. I could have gotten everything because I am a Reyes, because I can buy anything...and everything, except Nena.

He had wanted not to think about her any more but it was impossible, not after Arrastequi had taunted him. Yes, he had known that most noble of sentiments, and the knowledge came to him long ago, long before he had acquired a taste for kippers for breakfast and anisado after dinner.

Nena was twelve when she came to the old house with those huge caryatids, a dozen polished mirrors and a hundred porcelain statues which his grandfather had gathered from cheap curio shops in Europe. She helped in the kitchen most of the time; she was a tenant's daughter and had come to work for the family. He had been attracted by her face, its precious serenity that evoked images of peace and forebearance. It was her face that attracted him most for it seemed to mirror a calm, even stoic, resignation and a capacity to endure and bear all pain. When he finally felt surer of himself, her portrait was the first he did. It was a small frame in oil and he kept it in his apartment afterwards as if it were some guardian angel whose benign presence dispelled from the house all the nagging wraiths of loneliness and exorcised the very air of its heaviness. And he remembered this always with a wry smile—he used to sit before the portrait and shake a finger at it, saying, "Nena, be true, be true!"

She did not stay in the kitchen always for his father sent her to school, "to be more useful" as he put it, and there were times when she did seek him for help in some of her housework, a chore which he gladly accepted because he could be near her, because he could feel the occasional warm brush of her arm on his and the caress of her breath on his neck as she stood behind him watching him deftly come out with the answers on her arithmetic pad.

When he left for England, where his father sent him when he was in his second year in high school, he had all but forgotten Nena although he remembered having received a letter or two from her. Then it really happened on his first vacation—a vacation he had looked forward to for that winter had been very bitter and a few pipes in the dormitory had burst when the water had frozen. It was late December when he reached Negros, the cane was green and tall as a man and it seemed as if life had meaning and was not circumscribed by a cold that had withered the leaves from the trees and banished the sun from a pewter sky. It was December, yes—but the sun was out, and sailed that afternoon across the fields and lingered beyond the foothills in a mass of fiery red. And because he was sixteen, because he was home, he had felt that there was nothing better than the sweet, juicy air of Negros. He tried out a new chestnut-colored pony which his father had added to the stable and rediscovered the farthest corner of the hacienda in the foothills, had galloped to the edge of the cogon forest and circled back in a wide arc that left the poor beast panting and tired. Dusk had come and he was slowly cantering home when he noticed this girl in tennis shoes walking ahead of him along the narrow, cane-flanked trail.

It was Nena returning from a visit to her folks and from a distance, he dismounted and walked quietly to her; from that distance, too, he noticed how tall she had become and was, as a matter of fact, even taller than he. It was the first time that she was alone with him, alone in this vast greenness of cane and grass and earth, while the sun died and scattered its last splendor upon the dimming sky above them. "You gave me a fright," she had said for she had turned with a start when he approached. It seemed as if she did not want to talk unless she was asked something so he said tentatively, feeling his way, "Do you want to ride home with me?"

She gave out a shy, little laugh and after that he knew he could tell her anything, anything, not just what he told her in the house when he wanted a helping of paella or another cup of ice cream. More than this, much more than this and so he started with London, the gray fog and the bitter cold that crept into his very bones; he told her of the boys in his school and their sense of fun, the few girls he had met, freckled, red-nosed and with pigtails, who were often demanding and frank. And without being aware of its implications, he had asked her if she had been in love and after some silence she said that she did not know and because it was getting dark and the wind that ruffled the canefields was cool, and because he was young and just home from England, he wheeled around, held her clumsily and touched her face. It came like the world's end, like the first intimation of knowledge—this burst of pealing by a thousand bells, this swath of pain across his face. Then he realized that she had broken free and had slapped him. And now, in the gathering dusk, she started to cry, her sobs small and broken and he could only make out the words, "just because...just because"...that was all, and he felt so small and so filled with shame he could have been swallowed by the earth and he wouldn't have cared for he had not really meant to defile her; not really—all he wanted was to touch her face.

Years afterwards when he remembered and he told her this, she was always silent and there would steal into him this indescribable ache, this desire to comfort her and be good to her, as if this was the only precious gesture he could show because none of his gifts, not his name or his heritage was enough barter for her surrender. She went to Manila with the family when his father decided to build a house in Pobres Park. He was going into politics and could not stay in the province because it was in Manila that all the power and the successful politicians were. He could not quite understand at first why they had to move to Manila. His father explained everything: he was not meant to be a politician, he was short and swarthy and did not have the speaking prowess of the politicios who harangued the crowd in their town plaza. But his father had to be in politics because their sugar interest must not only be protected, it must be preserved. Sugar was in the family, in the blood—it was the only thing the Reyeses knew, it was the only crop they planted and nurtured. They talked sugar and tariffs, sugar and prices; sugar and new markets, sugar and nationalism until anything of sugar repelled him. When he returned to Manila after finishing Form One, Nena was no longer a gangling farm girl; she was a handsome woman, sure of herself and what she could do. Furthermore, she could talk sugar for she had become an asset to his father; she was now one of his secretaries.

Arrastequi came early as he had promised and they breakfasted on grapes, brown bread, chorizos, a pitcher of warm milk and coffee. When they stepped out, the sun had broken free from the low ring of pine-covered hills that surrounded Marquina. It glinted on the red brick and on the faded escutcheons at the doorways.

With Arrastequi, there were only two subjects that deserved attention: pelota and women, and the latter seemed more important. Two future pelotaris—boys in short pants—asked Arrastequi if he could play with them but he waved them off. They got into the Ford and the Spaniard started his never-ending dissertation on women again. "Ah, Manila—you have a lot of homely women but the pretty ones, chico—they are pure heaven. And you know something? Your women have a nobility which other women don't have. They are true, they are faithful. American women—bah! Mexican, Cuban—they drop you once you no longer have money. It's not so with Filipino women. No—I am not talking of my woman, of course, because while she is faithful to me, she has not been faithful to her husband"—a loud laugh—"But she's an exception. Filipino women are loyal and true like Spanish women."

Hearing the Spanish talk of fidelity as if it was a virtue monopolized by Filipinos, in his own dark mind, he thought again of Nena—the vacillating between belief and unbelief, the giddy rationalizations with which he had hoped to banish all doubts. She didn't die because of what I have done—she took her life away not because of me but because of an inner compulsion, a terrible sense of guilt that she debased not only her life but mine. And she died not because she was faithful, not because there was anything sacred we had defiled but because she wanted to prove that in destroying her life, she was creating a new one—not in her corpse but in me whom she had left to walk the streets and breathe the sordid air.

How easy it was to believe that this was so but it was not, and inwardly, he envied his father who had never been bothered by such meanderings of the mind; he envied his mother, too, who confirmed his hopes, who showed enough grit to be above his father's profligacies even when these were dumped at her very door.

His father—how his sensuality and his barbaric insensitiveness rankled every time he remembered. But in time, he had come to accept his father's sins as inevitable in the social order of Negros. He couldn't remember a single man of his father's stature or acquaintance who did not have a mistress or two either in the farm, in Bacolod or in the city—sometimes the innocent daughter of a tenant as if this, too, was foreordained. Once his father brought to the house this mestiza from Manila who was young enough to be his daughter and she lived with them for a month, ate at the table and joined them even in the evening prayers after which she retired to her room with his father in tow like a dog. Pepe knew, his sisters knew, his mother knew but they were silent and meek and his mother bore it all with pride and regal disdain as if it never happened, as if it was some nightmare that would pass. She could have told him how she felt because they were close to each other, because their relationship was characterized by warmth and small confidences. But she did not, although, of course, he could very well understand how she felt. On the morning that his father finally took the woman to the boat that would take her to Manila and oblivion, his mother called him to her room. He had expected her to tell him. There was every reason for her to have been bitter for the vestiges of her suffering were now delible in her battered face, swollen lips and bruised arms. He had gathered her in his arms and cried and she had stroked his head then turned to her huge dressing mirror and studied her face. "I am growing old, Pepe," she moaned, "I am not young any more, you can see that. Four children—and oh so many worries. Look at the blemishes on my skin and the bulges on my arms and hips. I must get rid of these. And you can't do these with cosmetics alone." And because he worshipped her, he assured her that she was lovely still, that she was more beautiful than all of his father's women. And on that day, he arranged to have a professional masseuse and a skin specialist fly to Negros every week and the treatment became a family institution when they moved to Manila because he could not bear to see her again as she was that morning.

What then is fidelity, how may one define it or recognize it in a pile of emotional evidence when it assumes chameleon colors and could easily be interpreted as no more than sheer, doggedness in one woman or inexplicable devotion in another?

With Nena he was not sure and herein—in this doubt lay the root of his malaise. In the end she showed him the supreme evidence but he was too concerned then with his own petty self to acknowledge it. He had picked her up that afternoon at the usual corner near his father's office then they drove down the Boulevard for merienda. After merienda, they went to his apartment where he always isolated himself when he left the house in Pobres Park. Here they could be alone, they could talk and plan—that was the most important thing—plan, as if there was a benign future to reap. Even after she had told him everything, she still retained an aura of inviolability which he had learned to appreciate because they did nothing more than kiss in the quiet intimacy of this room. This was what Nena had wanted and he did not ask for more, just this—the luxury of being alone with her and being able to tell her all the hankerings that flitted across his mind, recall the days in Negros when she was twelve and her skin was darker and her hands were rough although even then, her eyes were luminous and bright. But he must ask her—there was no sense holding on to a myth because now he was sure that the filth was real and not a creation of his idle mind. But how must one start? How tell Nena that she was deceitful? And if she was, did it really matter? He was, after all, willing to marry her no matter what had happened and he would have gladly done all she wanted done if she only accepted him.

His room was decorated to his taste and it was austere compared to his father's office which was heavily carpeted and draped with vermillion. It was paneled with dao. He had a view of the bay and the wide glass windows were opened to the salt air and the distant thrum of traffic. He had built this small house with his mother's assistance and here, but for an old couple from Negros who looked after the house and the garden, he was alone. This was his sanctuary from the house in the park: it had no telephone and none of his friends had been to it—no one except his mother and Nena. She had primmed before the mirror; she was tall and brown and there was a girlishness in the way she did her hair. When she turned to speak to him, he looked into her eyes, saw once more the quality of forebearance in them. He went to her, held her face and brought her warm, moist lips to his. "You have always been honest with me," he said. "And I have never asked questions." She had looked at him and her eyes shone as she murmured, "I love you," softly, warmly. How wonderful it was to hear her say it, to wallow in the grace of those words and forget the tenacious and aching doubt. But he wanted to be sure and the question was a statement, a conclusion that was as true as sunrise. "I saw you last night with him. I felt so utterly betrayed..." She jerked away and a cry, anguished and surprised, broke from her. He had followed her to the window. Beyond the ebony strip of the boulevard was the pale blue sea, and above the sea, the sun embroidered the sky with splashes of indigo and red. It would be dark soon and already the mercury lamps of the boulevard glistened with a hard metallic sheen. When she turned to him again, her eyes were misty. But she spoke calmly: "I knew that there would be a time like this. I have lived in fear of your knowing. Believe me, I would have stopped if I could help it. But it's too late. I was marked out for this, long ago before you and I were born."

"Is it as final as that?" She had nodded and could not look at him. "Your father can tell me to do anything he wants but he does not possess my will. There are reasons...and you know what they are." Her voice trembled. "Oh God, there's always a reason. And it's so easy for others to make conclusions,"—she turned to him and her face was pale: "You have a place like this and there's that farm and that house in Pobres Park." She went to him and thrust her face at him: "Ask me—ask me anything. What else do you want to know about me?" Then she broke down and the animal intensity of her sobbing shook her and seemed to drain her of all strength. When she was quiet again, he gathered her in his arms and fondled her hair. Afterwards: "I could have told you everything—when I was younger. But I was selfish, I guess. I wanted to make believe that it was possible although I knew it was not."

"It is still possible."

"Pepe," she had said. "It is not. And I cannot ask you to forgive me. There is nothing to forgive and it does not make any difference because I have told you." She clung to him and her voice was hoarse, "It was impossible from the beginning."

Now the mind rolled back to treasured images, an old-fashioned kitchen with a huge charcoal stove, canefields stretching like a carpet of lustrous green to the hills, and a girl shyly saying in a few moments stolen from the bustle of farewell at the pier, "Write to me about England..."

"What matters," he had heard her dimly, "what really matters is that I am true. With you, I was not concerned with myself, my family or my responsibility. With you, I was myself and I didn't ask for anything..."

She did not ask for anything. All that she wanted was to know if he was well, if he was healthy and happy, and he said, "I have nothing to share with you. I have nothing of my own. Not my father's wealth. The only precious things I have are you and my mother..."

"Your mother?" incredulously.

"Yes. You don't believe it?"

"No," she said simply. "She is no different, I know."

"Don't talk that way about her."

She clung to him again. "What do you want me to tell you then?"

"The truth."

"It doesn't matter any more. You'll only hate me more."

"I want to know just the same."

After a long silence: "You were in England."

"It couldn't be helped," he said.

"I was sixteen. I couldn't do anything. I expected it. My parents expected it. It turned out to be for the good of all of us—more so when he took me to Manila to work. And I was not the only one."

He held her close.

"I'm lucky, I guess," she had said flatly, drawing away. Her eyes were no longer misty but the traces of grief were still in her tear-stained face. "Yes, I am lucky. Not many would have the chances I now have. And look at my brothers and sisters—they are all going to college and one is already a nurse..."

"There's always a reason."

"Don't be too harsh with me," she said. "It is easy for you to make conclusions. You can say a million people should be marched off to the wall. You can go around with your fancy crowd, doing as you please. You can afford it, you have never known fear or sorrow. And that is why you can be brave..."

"And my father?"

"In a way, he has many good qualities. Without him..."

He could not hide his contempt. "He is a leader, he is a nationalist...he aspires for the highest office of the land. But he is a crook, a lecher, and he will sell his country down the river because everyone lets him get away with it..."

She shook her head. "He is still your father. You will be a Reyes all your life..." The hopelessness of it all engulfed him and yet, he should have expected this. How many times had they been together, just the two of them? And who would believe that he hadn't taken her as a man should take a woman. There was no one who could see, there were just the two of them who understood what she was saying now, "This is the reason I haven't...With you, it is different."

"Can we start all over again?"

She said, "You cannot take my brain and wash it,"

"What can I do then?"

"You can kill your father," she said with a nervous laugh and for a moment, he was sure he could do it, too, not only for Nena or his mother but for himself.

"Or you can go away and not see me any more," she added quickly. "Best choice, I can kill myself and that would end your problem."

"You fool," he had said, hugging her. But even as he spoke he had already made up his mind and decided to leave Manila, and all its wretched people.

Their first stop was at Cenaruzza where they gazed at the bronze statue of Simon Bolivar then they strode to the church across the square—an ancient edifice with sagging, roughhewn wooden beams and cracked, moss-covered walls. The church smelled of damp earth and rotting corners as do all the old churches in Spain. Arrastequi's knowledge of churches and history was rudimentary and he was not aware of what Bolivar had accomplished, nor did he possess a repertoire of interesting minutia about the church. His eyes lighted up, however, when he saw the fronton beyond the church and a crowd of boys who had broken up to meet them. "You see," he said expansively, "the pelota is the national sport of the Basque. It is dangerous, of course, but we love danger and if you start young, you will soon learn how to live with danger too." Again, the boys wanted him to play.

As they drove on, Arrastequi's talk returned to Jai Alai and his woman in Manila. "It was so simple, my meeting her. That restaurant in the Jai Alai—I was going in for a cup of coffee before getting in the fronton to practice. She was there with half a dozen girls, all of them not so young any more. One I knew very well and she introduced me to all of them and my woman—pardon me for not telling you her name—I want to protect her. She's from Negros and in spite of all the years she had lived in Manila, she had never seen Jai Alai. I told her I would be very happy to show her anytime and so she decided to stay—just she—so she could watch me. That's how it started. Simple, eh? I wanted to take her home afterwards—I didn't have a car and so she gave me this car...that was much later, of course, when we became friendly, shall we say. But I had to leave because trouble was coming. And her husband, he's rich—a sugar planter and politician. When I left, no one knew. You know, she is no longer young. Past forty—but she's well preserved. Her eyes—chinita, and her skin—it's milk and roses. I didn't tell her I was leaving too..."

He, too, did not tell anyone he was leaving for he had planned his departure to create a mild rampage in the ranks of the vultures of Pobres Park. Earlier, for two months, he had kept to himself in his retreat and worked on a hundred canvases. He painted with pleasure and premeditation the huge blobs of black and white, the yellows and the greens, the "phantoms" and "plastic enigmas" with which the pretentious art critics who coddled him had labeled his work. When he opened his show, he was surprised not at the variety of what he had done but at the turnout of people, the asses who accepted what he had dashed off, who even proclaimed the maturity of his art. But in the most recondite recesses of his mind, Pepe was aware of his limitations and the absence of true greatness in his bones. He sold them all, his cars, his bric-a-brac and other possessions so that there was almost nothing left in his house except a few books and Nena's portrait. His friends asked why he was doing this and he said he was beginning all over again not only his life but his art. And as the day approached, he felt more light-hearted and it seemed as if he was being cured of the last ravage of a disease and all that he had to do now was to lift the scab to be rid of everything, of anguish and of memory itself. He saw Nena for a few times but the meetings were casual. And on his last day, he invited all his friends. They came by the droves to congratulate him on his show; they were all there in one happy company—the culture-seekers, the mourners who lamented a past that did not stud the country with ancient artifacts and monuments of a superior civilization, the ladies who talked art because it was fashionable—they all wandered about his father's house, guzzling his liquor and murmuring platitudes.

He was most surprised when Nena showed up for he did not invite her. She went to him at once, "I know you are up to something. Inviting all these people." It was sheer masochism to ignore her, to flee the magic of her presence. In this thrall of evening, he could not really leave, could not be released from the formidable chains that bound them both, this kinship, knowledge, and this hating which united them because hate did not affirm, did not give birth to some nobility of the spirit, because hate did not edify. It destroyed.

He turned around to his guests; they had spilled out into the trim lawn lighted with Japanese lanterns, to the very rim of the swimming pool, opaque and placid in the glow. A couple was doing a cha-cha under the porte cochere at the end of the terrace, and others were dancing in the living rooms. Then, someone by the pool got a little exuberant and there was a splash, a sudden crowding there, and laughter and cheers when he joined them. He found his champion and art critic—a stodgy professor grinning ear to ear—in the water. He stepped to the edge of the pool, leaned over and extended his hand, a slight shove and then the surprise and shock as he hit the water. When his feet could not touch the bottom, in his numbed mind, the thought came clearly: this is how it feels to drown. Now there was nothing but this cavern of water which was swallowing him up. As the water closed about him, with that primordial instinct for survival, he flailed his arms and kicked. It was ages before a hand grabbed him from behind and hauled him to the shallow part of the pool. And when he was on his feet again, and able to wobble to the edge, he heard: "I hope you haven't drunk too much water," and he turned to see Nena, dripping wet, and smiling. It was she who had jumped in after him.

Much later, when they were in his old room and he had drunk the coffee which she had made, he noticed how lovely she was in his mother's robe even when her hair hung about her face in wet straggles. She was looking at him amusedly. "It may take sometime for your dress to dry," he had said; "Mama's clothes fit you—you can put on one and she won't mind."

"I am not in a hurry." She stood up and went to the window. On the lawn, under the lanterns, the crowd was still enjoying itself but there were no more dunkings in the pool.

"How does it feel to be a boy scout?" he asked.

She turned around and had bussed him on the chin. "They thought you were acting and they were applauding. I told you once you must learn how to swim and tomorrow I must teach you. This may be the only thing I can teach you."

"There's no tomorrow."

"There you go again."

"Thank you just the same. I'll remember you in my will."

"You don't have to give me anything," she said lightly. "Give it to someone else—an English girl, someone from the Continent or from Pobres Park..." Yes, it would have been vastly similar if it was some Continental bitch who had attracted him and lured him to stay, if in his wandering he had stumbled across some pit and never risen again but the pit was here, in this loathesome city. "I hate everything here," he said without bitterness.

"This is your home."

"My home?" he asked. "Does that mean anything? Listen. What

I like to do is to go back to Negros and live in that old house in the farm. You come with me. I want to sit in the balcony and watch the clouds crown the hill. That was wonderful..."

She interrupted him. "For you, yes. But not for me. It never was and never will be." He did not ask her to explain and afterwards, remembering her very words, he felt that he really understood her then.

Arrastequi handled the big Ford with consummate skill and it sang on the curves of the narrow mountain road. With a flourish of horns, they whistled through Basque villages and isolated farm houses; the patches of wheat astride the low hills were ripening into a golden yellow and the air was scented with the aroma of pine and grass. The sun blazed down and polished every living or inanimate thing—be it bullcarts plodding to the farms or bare scraggy granite—with a luminosity that dazzled the eye.

They reached Guernica before noon and they went up a dirt road astride the hill that overlooked the city. The cool wind refreshed the lungs, and they looked down upon a pattern of red tile and a church which was spared during the Civil War. Beyond the rooftops were the quilt-work farms that straddled the other hills.

"Was the whole city destroyed?"

"Yes," Arrastequi said. "Totally—but for the cathedral and a few houses. We were on the other side."

"You have seen Manila and the Walled City. The Walled City was also destroyed. All of it."

"It was a useless war," Arrastequi said. "And a costly one. My father fled to France, across the Pyrenees. There are still several exiles in France today. Many have returned. Paris is a wonderful place for exiles."

"I know," Pepe said. "I have a place there myself and that's where I will go when I leave Spain..."

They drove down the hill into the town, past the quiet streets, then stopped before an old building shaded with red beech and sycamores. They went in and looked at the darkened meeting place of the Basque rulers and the mementos of those days when the Basque were masters of their land. But as usual, Arrastequi knew little and soon, his thoughts were drifting to Manila again.

"You know," the pelotari said. "I have never written to her. It is difficult and I must be kind. But when I was in Manila she said she usually went to Paris in the fall. I will meet her there, of course, if I know when. I have grown to like her very much. Chico, you cannot have a woman like that who gives everything...And Paris in the fall, it's somber but it is lovely too."

It was his father who introduced him to Paris when he was finally through with Form One. The hacendero had gone to England and had taken him to Paris for a week, "to sample some adult male pleasures" as a requisite for his growing up and, in his father's words, as his graduation present. They stayed in a small hotel near the Place Du Trocadero and occupied a room each although it would have been cheaper for them to have taken just one room. It was something which he could not understand till towards evening when, before dinner, his father left him in his room and told him to wait—he would be away just for an hour and that he had a surprise for him. When he returned, his father was wreathed with smiles and there was something mischievous in his dark, porcine face. "I have a surprise for you at the door," he had said, and there she was, a trim blonde about his age. "Don't worry—she is clean," was all he said. "And as for me, I can take care of myself."

He had left them just like that and the girl who spoke a little English went to him and said she was his for the night, so would he start now or should they go out and have dinner then hurry back to the room? He had been terribly embarrassed not so much by the girl but at what his father had done, but the girl was quite understanding and she did not hurry or make unnecessary demands. They lay awake a good measure of the night, talking quietly afterwards while below them, the sounds of Paris died down and there was only this feeling that his initiation was not his alone but something which his father in his usual benevolence and magnanimity had shared. In the morning when his father woke him up, there was an ache in his bones. The girl was taking a shower and in the harsh light of day, he loathed facing his father, seeing his gloating face, hearing his throaty voice. But he stood up obediently and opened the door to let his father in. He was grinning widely, he was pleased with the world and with him was his woman—a girl as young as she who had shared his bed. "Well, I am glad that you are up early," his father had said. "I am sure that with your youth, you can do more than I...If you are not happy with her"—he thrust a chin at the shower, "I can bring you another."

"No, Papa," he said, his face burning all over. "I am contented with her."

He had slapped him on the shoulder, then sailed out to the street. Later, when the girl returned from the shower showing off her firm breasts and her clean, tawny flanks, he felt all desire ebb away and in its place was this revulsion and total rejection of what had happened. For the first time, he knew what it was to hate oneself and, "Get out of here," he calmly told her.

He was, of course, much wiser now and in those times that he passed the hotel, he always recalled that first knowledge with a wisp of sadness and wished that it hadn't happened that way for he had more than a special fondness for Paris, particularly in the fall.

After Manila, Paris had been his first stop and Paris in autumn was, indeed, hypnotic in its loveliness. The air was perfumed and there were chestnuts roasting on the sidewalk. It was a season which he appreciated because it was a soothing anodyne for all cares, a seductive twilight that seemed to befall all emotions and make them hazy or indistinct and, thus, for a season, bearable. He did not stay in the Place du Trocadero; he had become enamored with a small room near the Sorbonne, with aimless walks near the University, and quiet talks with acquaintances he had made—students and artists who had found in Paris a measure of freedom from the constrictions of whatever country they were in exile from. He had managed to bring some money with him and he never wrote home for it. He avoided the Filipinos whose geography of Paris was confined to its burlesque houses and fleshpots. But no matter how hard he tried to keep from them as if they were carriers of some incurable disease, he was not successful. Once, while window shopping at the Champs Elysees, along the cobbled sidewalk before the Pampam Cafe, a woman called out: "Pepe, Pepe!" He tried not to notice but this woman rushed up to him—one of the young matrons in Pobres Park whose name he couldn't recall—and pulled him to the table which she shared with two girls, most probably college graduates or friends who were on a shopping spree in the Continent. He reverted to his old trick of appearing obnoxious; he kissed the woman's hand and, at the same time, disparaged her for her provincial looks, ended the nastiness by suggesting that, perhaps, all of them would appreciate Paris better if each shared his bed, or better still, all three of them at the same time. They had all blushed, then recovered their composure and smiled gaily at his insolence and knowing perhaps, of his unusual ways, they started to humor him and were genuinely sorry when he bade them good-bye and, as a final fillip, he told them he was broke and would they please lend him fifteen dollars so that he wouldn't starve during the week? They parted—the money in his hands, the women giggling and saying they would let his mother know they saw him.

"What mother?"

"Conchita Reyes," they had chorused.

"I am not a Reyes and I don't have a mother," he said seriously. Indeed, it was the easiest thing to do in Paris, to pretend that he was not a Reyes, that his father was not an outstanding nationalist senator, that he was an artist and his sensibilities were more acute than those of the common riff-raff, particularly those in his own clan. The independence, the feeling that he was on his own was invigorating. He could now afford the high cost of freedom and his name need not be Reyes. In his first month in Paris, he took a clerking job in a bookstore on the Left Bank and put to use the scant knowledge of French which he learned in England. He could even live on his salary by skimping. He enjoyed the anonymity, wallowed in it, but one afternoon, a Filipino traced him to the shop and asked him to please come to the Embassy for there were letters for him and the ambassador would like to see him too. Again, his father's loving hand had reached out to him.

It was spring then; a harsh winter was over. The chestnut trees were in bloom, the flowers adorned the trees with white and even the grass seemed greener. At first he had not wanted to go but in a moment of homesickness, he did. A pile of mail awaited him and on the way home, in the metro, he went over his mother's letters first. The first, written two days after he had left Manila, told casually of Nena "...and you know, that girl, what had she eaten?

She slashed her wrists yesterday and didn't even think of us, your father, her family...Dearest Pepe, I know why she did it. She did not tell, but I know...and now, more than ever, I am worried about you. Please come home. Please let me know how you are..."

The days that followed were a desolate and trackless haze. It was now his conviction that he was responsible for her death which would, henceforth, loom over his life like a pall. In the afternoons when his turn at the bookshop was over, he no longer tarried by the other bookshops or galleries. In the confines of his room, he would lie and close his eyes, envision her face, the quiet assurance of her arms around him, the honeyed taste of her lips, the remembered fragrance of her hair. In the depths of him, she wasn't dead; she was with him always and there was no way by which these fond images would be wrenched from his mind. He could die, of course, and death was always the last reality and escape, the abyss he couldn't measure, whose rim he couldn't touch because it moved away from him when he thought he was near it. It could satisfy his greatest need, this last sanctuary where all were equal, where in eternal darkness there was no love or hatred, because in this pit no light filtered in, no smell—nothing but silence and ambiguity and all the secrets that cannot be probed. Did God walk its depths or, perhaps, if God could speak, could He tell—could He, perhaps, in His infinite goodness let two people, just two people meet again?

"So, if you have a place in Paris, give the address to me and I will introduce her to you," Arrastequi said.

"You should go back to Manila."

"If I can, chico. Yes, if I can," Arrastequi said solemnly. "Even if I didn't meet this woman, I would like to go there. To make my home there. That's the country of the future. Everyone can be President."

He had begun to like the Spaniard. Arrastequi's affection for the Philippines—this stirred not only curiosity but self-doubt; it was possible that, after all, he could have looked at his country from an extremely narrow perspective. He did not want this doubt to grow and it was, therefore, absolutely necessary now that he must leave Marquina. Another moment with Arrastequi would bring him nearer to Manila.

Arrastequi offered, "All right, I'll drive you to San Sebastian. You can slip into your swimming trunks when we get there and just walk to the beach and swim. But don't go too far out. There's a dangerous undertow and it is deep. Then, in the evening, you can take the train to Paris."

It was a generous gesture and he was beginning to feel attached to the pelotari in spite of his loud-mouthed boasting.

They started out after another heavy breakfast and loaded his two suitcases in the trunk of the car. The morning was scented and the sun shone brilliant and serene on the sycamores, on the grass and the gray stone. In the fronton, boys in shorts were already gathered for the daily ritual and the sound of the leather ball hitting the board reached them like intermittent pistol shots. There was no traffic save an occasional oxcart loaded with pine logs or compost.

When they got to the highway, Arrastequi became voluble again. The drive was smooth and lavished with little surprises; a turn along the eucalyptus-studded hillsides and the sea opened up to them, dark blue and shimmery, and down the dip, among the rocks and the yellow thrust of wildflowers, the red roof of a solitary house or a fisherman's cove, his boat beached on a narrow strip of golden sand.

Arrastequi was careful and he managed the curves with diffidence. They stopped once at a roadside farm where the family was plowing, the father managing the oxen and the mother and the children trailing the plow and spreading compost on the newly-turned soiled. Wheat was ripening in some of the farms and the grain covered the hillsides with patches of yellow. On the narrow plain to San Sebastian, the road widened and the traffic became dominated by French cars; it would be mid-summer soon and the coast would be teeming with vacationists.

"Oh, I haven't told you a most interesting incident which shows how broadminded she is." Arrastequi continued reminiscing. "Ah—she was willing to share me with others. Maybe, she just wanted me to be happy, to do a little hunting while the hunting was good."

"I don't get you," Pepe said. Again, his curiosity was aroused.

"Well," Arrastequi said, smacking his lips, "One day, she

116

introduced me to two of her friends—young married women, and pretty too. She said I could visit them—visit them, mind you, and that I did. Oh, it was all carefully planned, of course. And how I enjoyed these visits. And you know, she never asked me how they turned out and I never told her because I wanted to spare her feelings..."

Arrastequi's talk had become boring and Pepe was relieved when they reached San Sebastian. They proceeded to the Old Quarter, to Arrastequi favorite restaurant which was tucked away in the basement of a dingy-looking building. The restaurant was just as decrepit-looking as its exterior but when the octopi and lobster came, all its poor appointments were forgotten.

They went back to the car after lunch and drove around the town, through narrow streets flanked by stone buildings that loomed dark and grim around them. When they reached the fishing quay, a few boats were docked, their nets strung on slender poles. Beyond the quay was the Playa de la Concha curving like a golden scimitar and on the right, the calm, blue sea. The sun poured on the sand, on the gray tile roofs of the buildings, on the red and green paint of the fishing boats.

"It is still cold—the water, but we can swim now." The pelotari pointed to a few bathers sunning themselves on the beach—"If they can endure the cold, we can."

"It doesn't matter really," Pepe said for he had no intention of swimming although he had a desire now to slip his trousers off and just lie on the sand. Arrastequi parked his car in the lot beside a posh, whitewashed hotel and they stripped.

They walked barefoot under the stunted tamarindo trees, down the broadwalk to the stone stairs which dropped into the beach.

Arrastequi spoke about his woman again: "You wouldn't think she had had four children," he shook his head. "But she has kept her figure. You should see her in a bathing suit. Filipino women seldom get fat even when they grow old. But look at our women, look at what balls of fat they become once they are past forty. Not her—chico."

"I don't know how she did it," Pepe said. "But if she is past forty and still has a figure, she must really have taken good care of herself."

"Not really," Arrastequi said, jumping onto the cool, soft sand. "She has gone to Japan for some beauty treatments. Twice I think. And she is visited regularly by a masseuse and a skin specialist..."

"A masseuse and a skin specialist?"

"Yes," the pelotari said. "Every week..."

"Every week?"

"Yes, I couldn't see her Tuesday afternoons. But on other days, ah—chico..."

"No," Pepe said aghast.

"You don't believe me? I can show you her picture when we get back to the car. But that is not important. I told you she lives in Pobres Park in that fancy house with a huge swimming pool. I have never been in it...that was impossible. It is not only social position which she has. And I am coming to that. The reason I had to leave the Philippines—run away, rather...I'm not boasting. But facts are facts. She is married to a very powerful man...a sugar planter. And you know, chico, they say her husband would be President someday. President, do you understand?"

"I understand," Pepe said brusquely, walking faster.

"What can a poor pelotari like me do then? I think he found out. We had been very careful..."

"And you ran away?"

"Yes, but I want to go back. Nothing like this ever happened to me before. So it is not love, so it is just passion. But chico, can you draw the line between passion and love?"

"There is a difference," Pepe said, fear and anxiety gripping him. "But I don't want to talk about it, and I don't want to hear any more about your woman. It's your damn business...not mine..."

"All right then," the pelotari said, a little hurt. "But do me a favor...just one favor. If you get back to Manila, please go see her and tell her to come to me. I cannot go to her—that's impossible. You understand, don't you?"

Pepe headed for the sea.

"You understand, don't you?" the pelotari followed him.

"I don't want to know anything more about her," Pepe said grimly.

"Look, Pepe, we are friends," the pelotari said. "I cannot write to her. That is why I am confiding in you. You can keep a secret—just this one secret..."

"No, I can't," Pepe said, breaking into a run.

Let him talk no more; God, close his mouth forever. I don't want to know, I don't want to know! But the pelotari was behind him, pursuing him, telling him the final word.

"Her husband is a senator. I can't afford to tarnish her name. You know what I am driving at."

Pepe fled but he could hear the pelotari's quickening footfall follow him.

"I don't want to hear any more. I don't want to hear," he cried and lashed out into the sea, away and into the water, into the waiting embrace of the sea. He must not hear, he must not know, and above the noise of the surf, whispering surf on the beach, he could not hear, he must hear no more of Manila or the encumbered past.

F. Sionil José's fiction has been published internationally and been translated into several languages, including his native Ilokano. He founded the Philippine Center of International PEN in 1958. In 1980 he received the Ramon Magsaysay Award for journalism, literature and creative communication arts. His allegory "Waywaya," which appeared in SSI No. 35, won first prize in the esteemed literary competition in the Philippines: the Annual Palanca Memorial Awards.

"...I realized that in spite of the crowded party
my movements had been closely monitored."

Reception

BY PAUL THEROUX

THE best telegram I ever had said this: CALL ME TOMORROW FOR
WONDERFUL NEWS. I had twenty hours to imagine what the news
might be. And I delayed for a few hours more. I wanted to prolong
the pleasure. I loved the expectation. How often in life do we have
the bright certainty that everything is going to be fine?

Traveling alone through Europe, I had just left Germany for
Holland, where the telegram awaited me. I liked the Dutch. They
were sensible; they had been brave in the war. They still tried to
understand the world, and their quaint modernism had made them
tolerant. They behaved themselves. It was a church-and-brothel
society in which there were neither saints nor sinners, only at worst
a few well-meaning hypocrites. Vice without passion, theology
without much terror; they were even idealistic in a practical way.
They were unprejudiced and open-minded without being naïvely
enthusiastic. They had nice faces. Their pornography was
ridiculous, and I think it embarrassed them, but they knew that left
to its impotent spectators and drooling voyeurs it was just another
sorry prop in sex's sad comedy.

In Amsterdam, where I could have chosen anything, I chose to be idle. I smoked a little hash, talked to Javanese in quacking Bahasa, and was reminded how the "colonial" and the "bourgeois" are full of the same worthy illusions, like the solidity and reassurance of plump upholstered armchairs in a warm parlor. I sat and read. I ate Eastern food and slept soundly in a soft Dutch bed. Each night I dreamed without waking—it had never happened in Ayer Hitam, where nights were rackety and hot.

It was winter. The canals froze. Some people skated, as they did in the oldest oil paintings on earth—moving so fast that the swipes of the speed-skaters' blades made a sound like knives being sharpened. Gulls dived between the leaning buildings and gathered on the green ice. The small frosty city smelled of its river and its bakeries, and beer. I went for long ankle-twisting walks down cobblestone streets.

At last, almost sad because it meant the end of a joyous wait, I made my phone call. The telegram had been informal—a friend in the State Department. I had tried to avoid guessing the news: expect nothing and you're never disappointed.

She said, "You've got London."

This was London, this reception. A month had passed since the telegram. The party invitations had my name on them ("To Welcome..."). The guests had been carefully selected—it was pleasure for them, a night out. For us, the embassy staff, it was overtime. I did not mind. I had wanted London. In London I could meet anyone, do anything, go anywhere. It was the center of the civilized world, the best place in Europe, the last habitable big city. It was the first city Americans thought of traveling to—funny, friendly, and undemanding; it was every English-speaker's spiritual home. I had been intending to come here for as long as I could remember.

And this was also a promotion for me: from FSO-5, my grade as consul in the Malaysian town of Ayer Hitam, to FSO-4, political officer. My designation was POL-1, not to be confused with POL-2, the CIA—"The boys on the third floor," as we called them at the London embassy. I was a spy only in the most general and harmless sense of the word.

It had been a mistake to walk from my hotel to this reception. My hotel was in Chelsea, near the Embankment; the party was at Everett Horton's Briarcliff Lodge, in Kensington. London is not a city. It is more like a country, and living in it is like living in Holland or Belgium. Its completeness makes it deceptive—there are sidewalks from one frontier to the other—and its hugeness makes it possible for everyone to invent his own city. My London is not your London, though everyone's Washington, D.C., is pretty much the same. It was three miles from my hotel to Horton's, and this was only a small part of the labyrinth. A two-mile walk through any other city would take you inevitably through a slum. But this was unvarying gentility—wet narrow streets, dark housefronts, block upon block. They spoke of prosperity, but they revealed nothing very definite of their occupants. They were sedate battlements, fortress walls, with blind windows or drawn curtains. I imagined, behind them, something tumultuous. I had never felt more solitary or anonymous. I was happy. The city had been built to enclose secrets, for the British are like those naked Indians who hide in the Brazilian jungle—not timid, but fanatically private and untrusting. This was a mazy land of privacies—comforting to a secretive person, offering shelter to a fugitive, but posing problems to a diplomat. It was my job to know its secrets, to inform and represent my government, to penetrate the city and make new maps.

That walk through London humbled me. I began to feel less like an adventurer—a grand cartographer—than someone in a smaller role. I played with the idea that we were like gardeners. We were sent to maintain this garden, to keep the grass cut and the weeds down, to dead-head the roses, encourage the frailer blossoms. We could not introduce new plants or alter it. We watched over it, kept it watered; we dealt with enemies and called them pests. But our role was purely custodial. Each of us, in time, would go away. It was the image of a harmless occupation.

But of course in London there was a difference. It was a city without front yards. This was not America, with a low-maintenance lawn around every house. The garden was not a boasting acre here to advertise prosperity to passersby. In London, all gardens were behind the houses. They were hidden. "Plots" was the word.

Briarcliff Lodge had once belonged to a duke. It rose up from its surrounding hedge, a graceful monument of creamy floodlit walls and tall windows. What an earlier age had managed with stone, we had with light—floodlights, spotlights, bulbs behind cornices and buried in the ground, wrapped in vines and under water. It was beauty as emphasis, but it also afforded protection. Inside and out, Everett Horton had restored Briarcliff Lodge at embassy expense. He had hired six waiters tonight, and two front-door functionaries. I handed the first my raincoat—apologizing for its being wet—and gave my name to the second man. But I was not announced. I was early and, after all, I was the guest of honor.

"Mr. Horton will be down shortly."

"Excuse me, where's the—?"

"Just behind you, sir. One flight up."

In such circumstances the British are telepathic.

Then I heard a child's voice from the upper floor.

"Are the people here yet, Dad?"

"Not yet, but they will be soon. Better make it snappy." It was Horton's voice. He cleared his throat and said, "Now, do you want to do a *tinkle* or a *yucky*?"

I began to back away.

"Both," the child said.

"All right," the diplomat said patiently. "Take your time."

All happy families have a private language. The Hortons' was just about as useful and ludicrous-sounding as any other. But if Horton could be that patient with his child, I had little to worry about; and if he was happy, he was more than human.

The rooms in this house were enormous—a gym-size drawing room (perhaps once the ballroom), a library, the dining room to the right, and behind it the morning room and conservatory. A foyer, a cloakroom, a wide staircase. And this was only the ground floor. It was ducal splendor, but Horton was no duke. He lived, I knew, with his wife and child in an apartment on the third floor, at the back of the house. Servants' quarters, really—their little yellow kitchen, microwave oven, dishwasher, toaster, Bloomingdale's furniture, their TV, and five telephones. Horton had not taken possession of the house—he was its custodian. He lived like any janitor, like any gardener. Such is the fate of a career diplomat.

Some minutes later, he came downstairs.

"We've got rather a mixed bag tonight," he said. He was formal, a bit stiff-faced. He had a reputation for affecting British slang, and it was hard for me now to think of him as the same man who had just said a *tinkle* or a *yucky.*

The front door thumped shut.

"Mr. and Mrs. Roger Howlett," said the functionary from the hall. There was both dignity and strain in his announcing voice.

"The publisher," I said.

"Good show," Horton said. "I'm glad you had a chance to swot up the guest list."

He was being tactful—I had done little else for the past week. It had been, so far, the whole of my job, that guest list with its fifty names—and more: occupations, ages, addresses, and (if applicable) political leanings. It was a comprehensive list, like "Cast of Characters" at the opening of a Victorian novel. Learning it was like cramming a vocabulary list for a language exam. The only danger at such a reception was in knowing too much—startling the innocent guest by seeming overfamiliar with him.

Until then, my overseas experience had been in Uganda and Malaysia. Prudence, but not much subtlety, had been required of me in those places. Uganda wanted money from us; Malaysia wanted political patronage. Both deviously demanded that we be explicit and suspected us of being spies. Here in London we were regarded as high-living and rather privileged diplomats, a bit spoiled and unserious. But in fact every officer at the London embassy was in his own way an intelligence gatherer. There were too many secrets here for any of us to be complacent. This garden was not ours, and it contained some strange blooms. And maybe all good gardeners are at heart unsentimental botanists.

Horton's drawing room was soon filled. I stood at the door to the foyer. In this, the most casual setting imaginable, no one could be blamed for thinking that mine was the easiest job in the world. But every American in that room was hard at work, and only the

British people here were enjoying themselves. Once again it struck me how cooperative party guests were—it was perhaps the only reason embassy receptions were ever given, to enlist the help of unsuspecting people to find out whether the natives were friendly, to take soundings, to listen for gossip.

I entered the room—penetrated London for the first time—and set to work.

"Hello. I don't think we've met," I said to a young woman.

It was Mrs. Sarah Whiting, second wife of Anthony Whiting, managing director of the British subsidiary of an American company that made breakfast cereal. Whiting himself was across the room, talking to Margaret Duboys from our Trade Section. The Whitings had no children of their own, though Mr. Whiting had three by a previous marriage to an American woman still resident in Britain and still referred to by Vic Scaduto, our CAO, as "Auntie Climax." Sarah Whiting was something of a mystery to the embassy; she had been married only a year to the managing director. She was still full of the effortful romance of the second marriage—or so it seemed. I got nowhere by inquiring about her husband's business. Second wives are usually spared the details: the husband's affairs were determined by another woman, long ago. Anyway, I knew the answers before I asked the questions.

She said, "You're an American."

"How did you guess?"

"You look as if you belong here."

"Seeing as how I've been here only a week, I'm deeply flattered."

"Then you must be the guest of honor," she said. "Welcome to London."

We chatted about the weather, the high price of apartments—I told her I was looking for a place—and the décor of this room. She spoke knowledgeably about interior decoration ("I would have done that fascia in peach"), and when I complimented her, she said that she was interested "in a small way." I was soon to find out how small.

"I make furniture," she said.

"Design or build it?"

"I do everything."

I was impressed. I said, "You upholster it, too?"

"Not much upholstery is necessary," she said. "Most of my furniture is for dollhouses."

I thought I had misheard her.

"You mean"—I measured a few inches with my fingers— "like this?"

"It depends on the house. Some are smaller, some bigger. I make cutlery, as well."

"For dollhouses?"

"That's right," she said.

"Very tiny knives and forks?"

"And spoons. And tea strainers. Why are you smiling?"

"I don't think I've ever met anyone in your line of work."

She said, "I quite enjoy it."

"Your children"—yes, I knew better, but it was the obvious next remark—"your children must be fascinated by it."

"It's not really a child's thing. Most of the collectors are adults. It's a very serious business—and very expensive. We export a great deal. In any case, I don't have any children of my own. Do you have kids?"

"I'm not married," I said.

"We'll find you a wife," she said.

I hated that—it was the tone of a procuress. I may have showed a flicker of disapproval, because she looked suddenly uneasy. Maybe I was queer! Bachelor means queer!

I said, "Please do."

She turned to the woman next to her and said, "Sophie, this is the guest of honor," and stepped aside to make room.

"Sophie Graveney," Sarah Whiting said, and introduced us.

Miss Graveney, thirty, was an Honorable, her late father a lord. Her brother had succeeded to the title. We knew little about her, except for the fact that she had spent some time in the States.

I said, "We were just talking about dollhouses."

"Sarah's passionate about them."

"If things go on like this, I'll have to get Sarah to rent me one to live in."

"You're looking for a place, are you?"

"Yes. Just an apartment—a flat."

"What location?"

"I'm near the river at the moment, near Chelsea Embankment. I think I'd like to stay down there."

"Chelsea's very nice. But it's pricey. You might find something in Battersea. It's not as fashionable, but it's just across the bridge—South Chelsea, the snobs call it. There are some beautiful flats on Prince of Wales Drive, overlooking the park."

"I'll consider anything except the sort of place that's described as 'delightfully old-fashioned.' That always means derelict."

"Those are lovely," she said. "Do you jog? Of course you don't, why should you?" And she gave me an appraising stare. She had soft curls and wore lip gloss and I could see her body move beneath her loose black dress. She was also very tall and had large feet. Her shoulders were scented with jasmine. "I do jog, though. For my figure. Usually around Battersea Park at the crack of dawn."

Sarah Whiting laughed and said, "Tell him your story about that man."

"Oh, God," Sophie said. "That man. Last summer I was out jogging. It was about seven in the morning and I'd done two miles. I was really mucky—pouring with sweat. An old man stepped in front of me and said, 'Excuse me, miss, would you care for a drink?' I thought he meant a drink of water. I was out of breath and sort of steaming. I absolutely stank. I could barely answer him. Then he sort of snatched at my hand and said, 'I've got some whiskey in my car.'"

Her eyes were shining as she spoke.

"Do you get it? There I am in my running shoes and track suit, drenched with sweat, my hair hanging in rat tails, and this foolish old man is trying to pick me up! At seven o'clock in the morning!"

"Incredible!" Sarah said.

"Then he said, 'I want to be your bicycle seat,' and made a hideous face. I jogged away," Sophie said innocently. "I didn't fancy him one little bit."

"If I get a flat near Battersea Park I can watch you jogging," I said.

"Yes. If you get up early. Isn't that thrilling?"

A waiter passed by with a tray of drinks. Sophie took another glass of white wine and, seeing that I did not take any, she looked somewhat disapproving.

"Oh, God, are you one of those people who don't drink?"

I said, "I'm one of those people who're cutting down."

"Oh, God, you don't smoke either—how boring! I smoke about two packs a day."

"Do you?" I said. "Now that's really interesting."

"Is that funny?" she said, and blinked at me. "I never know when people are joking."

There was a dim suspicion in her voice and a moment of stillness, as if she had just realized that I was a perfect stranger, who might be mocking her. She looked around and smiled in relief.

"Terry!" she said, as if calling for help.

She had seen a friend. She introduced him to me as Lord Billows, though he insisted I call him Terry. I recognized him from the guest list—he ran a public relations firm that had a New York office. We talked for the next ten minutes about smoking, its hazards and pleasures: he represented a tobacco company and was very defensive about its sponsorship of mountain-climbing competitions—teams of climbers racing up mountainsides, a sport I had never heard of. To change the subject, I told him I had spent the past two years in Malaysia. He said he knew "Eddie Pahang." Very chummy: he was referring to the Sultan of Pahang.

Lord Billows said, "Your ambassador in K.L. gave marvelous parties."

"So they said. I seldom got to K.L. I was in Ayer Hitam, with the stinking durians and the revolting rubber-tappers. You've never heard of it. Nobody has. On the good days it was paradise."

"Who was your sultan?"

"Johore."

"Buffles—I knew him well. Buffles was a real old trooper. A magnificent polo player in his time, you know. And a greatly misunderstood man."

"He used to come to our club once a year," I said. "One of his mistresses was in the drama society. She was a Footlighter. That's what they called themselves. They loved being in plays."

Lord Billows had been grinning impatiently at me through all this. Then he said, "I'm going to ask you a very rude question," and fixed his face against mine. "But you probably won't consider it rude. You Americans are so straight-forward, aren't you?"

"That is rather a rude question," I said.

Lord Billows said, "That's not the question."

"Ask him," Sophie said. "I'm all ears."

"The question is, are you in fact a member of a club in London?" Lord Billows turned aside to Sophie and said, "You see, in the normal way one would never ask an Englishman that."

I said, "I think the Ayer Hitam Club has a reciprocal arrangement with a London club."

"I doubt that very much," Lord Billows said. "I have three clubs. The Savile might suit you—we have some Americans. I'm not as active as I'd like to be, but there it is. I put your chap Scaduto up for the Savile. I could do the same for you. Let me give you lunch there. You could look it over. I think you'd find it convivial."

"Is it delightfully old-fashioned?" Sophie asked.

"Exactly," Lord Billows said.

Sophie said, "He'll detest it."

"When applied to houses, delightfully old-fashioned means a drafty ruin. When applied to clubs, it means bad food and no women."

"The Savile has quite decent food," Lord Billows said. "And most of the staff are women."

"I was in a club like that once," I said.

"In London?"

"The States. When I was eleven years old," I said. "No girls. That was the rule."

Lord Billows stared at me for several seconds, as if translating what I had said, and then he said coldly, "You'll excuse me?" He walked away.

"You shouldn't have said that to him," Sophie said. "Why make a fuss about men's clubs? I don't object. I hate all this women's lib stuff, don't you?"

She had not addressed the question to me, but to Mrs.

Howlett—Diana—wife of Roger, the publisher, who was standing next to her. The two women began laughing in a conspiratorial way, and Roger Howlett told me several stories about Adlai Stevenson, and I gathered Horton had briefed him about me, because Howlett finished his Stevenson stories by saying, "Adlai was enormously good value—single, like yourself."

"Meet Walter Van Bellamy," Roger Howlett said, and tapped a tall rangy white-haired man on the arm. "One of your fellow countrymen."

Bellamy showed me his famous face and celebrated hair, but his eyes were wild as he said, "You and I have an awful lot in common, sir." Then he moved away, pushing through the crowd with his arms up, like a sleepwalker.

"He won all the pots and pans last year," Howlett said. "And here is one of our other authors." He took hold of a large pink man named Yarrow.

"I've written only one book for Roger," Yarrow said. "It was political. About land reform. I was a Young Communist then. You didn't blink. That's funny—Americans usually do when I say that. It was a failure, my literary effort."

"I've found," Howlett said, "that some of my authors actually get a thrill when their books fail. I've never understood it. Is it the British love of amateurism?"

I knew from the guest list that Yarrow was a member of Parliament, but to be polite I asked him what his business was.

He hooked his thumb into his waistcoat pocket and sipped his drink and said, "I represent a squalid little constituency in the West Midlands."

The way he said it, with a smirk on his smooth pink face and a glass in his hand and his tie splashed—he had sloshed his drink as he spoke—I found disgusting. If he meant it, it was contemptible; if he had said it for effect, it was obnoxious.

I said, "Maybe you'll be lucky and lose your seat at the next election."

"No fear. It's a safe Tory seat. Labour haven't got a chance. The working class don't vote—too lazy."

"I want him to do me a book about Westminster," Howlett said.

"Europe—that's the subject. We're European," Yarrow said. "That's where our future is. In a united Europe."

"What actually is a European?" I asked. "I mean, what language does he speak? What flag does he salute? What are his politics?"

"Don't ask silly questions," Yarrow said. "I must go. There's a vote in the Commons in twenty minutes. Rather an important bill."

"Are you for it or against it?"

"Very much against it!"

"What is the bill?"

"Haven't the faintest," Yarrow said. "But if I don't vote, there'll be hell to pay."

He left with two other MPs. Howlett went to the buffet table, and I walked around the room. I saw Miss Duboys talking to Lord Billows, and Vic Scaduto to Walter Van Bellamy, the poet. A black American, named Erroll Jeeps, from our Economics Section, looked intense as he stabbed his finger into the transfixed face of a woman. Jeeps saw me passing and said, "How are you holding up?"

"Fine," I said.

"This is our main man," Jeeps said, "the guest of honor."

I said, "I'd almost forgotten."

"It's a very jolly party," the woman said. "I'm Grace Yarrow."

"I just met your husband."

"He's gone to vote. But he'll be back," she said.

"The third reading of the finance bill," Jeeps said. "It's going to be close."

"You Americans are so well informed," Mrs. Yarrow said.

Horton stepped over and said, "I'm going to drag our guest of honor away," and introduced me to a *Times* journalist, an antique dealer named Frampton, and a girl who did hot-air ballooning. The party had grown hectic. I stopped asking for names. I met the director of a chain of hotels, and then a young man who said, "Sophie's been telling me all about you"—as if a great deal of time had passed and I had grown in reputation. A party was a way of speeding friendship and telescoping time. It was a sort of hothouse concept of forced growth. We were all friends now.

Someone said, "It rains every Thursday in London."

"We bought our Welsh dresser from a couple of fags," someone else said.

The man named Frampton praised one of Horton's paintings, saying, "It's tremendous fun."

At about eleven, the first people left, and by eleven-thirty only half the guests remained. They had gathered in small groups. I met a very thin man who gave his name as Smallwood, and I could hardly match him to the man on the guest list who appeared as Sir Charles Smallwood. And I assumed I had the wrong man, because this fellow had a grizzled, almost destitute look and was wearing an old-fashioned evening suit.

Edward Heaven, a name that appeared nowhere on the guest list, was a tall white-haired man with large furry ears, who vanished from the room as soon as he told me who he was, on the pretext of giving himself an insulin injection in the upstairs toilet. "Puts some people off their food, it does," he said, but he made for the front door, and the next moment he was hurrying down the street in the drizzle, without a coat.

The party was not quite over, I thought. But it was over. Of the nine people remaining in the room, seven were embassy people, and when the last guests left—the *Times* man and the antique dealer—Horton said to us, "Now, how about a real drink?"

He then went out of the room and told the hired help they could go home. In his dark suit, and carrying a tray, Horton looked like a waiter. On the tray was a bottle of whiskey and some glasses. He poured himself a drink, urged us to do the same, and said, "Please sit down—this won't take long."

I assumed this was one for the road. But it occurred to me, sitting among my embassy colleagues, that I had said very little to them all evening. In a sense, we were meeting for the first time. Their party manner was gone, and although they were tired—it was well past midnight—they seemed intense, all business. This impression was heightened by the fact that Debbie Horton, Everett's wife, had disappeared upstairs in the last hour of the party. Neither Miss Duboys nor I was married, and none of the others' wives were present. We had all come to the reception alone.

Horton sat in the center of the circle of chairs, like a football coach after an important game. Scaduto had told me that he liked to be called "coach." He looked the part—he was a big fleshy-faced man, who used body English when he spoke.

He said, "To tell the truth, I didn't expect to see Lord Billows here tonight. We were told he was going through a rather messy divorce."

"They've agreed on a settlement," Al Sanger said. Sanger had dark hair and a very white face and a bright, almost luminous, scar on his forehead. He was, like me, a political officer, but concerned with legal matters. "His wife gets custody of the children."

Miss Duboys said, "What happens to her title?"

"She stays Lady Billows," Erroll Jeeps said. "If she remarries, she loses it."

"Find out what she's styling herself now," Horton said to Jeeps. "We don't want to lose touch with her. If we do, there goes one of our most persuasive strings." He turned to me and said, "I noticed our guest of honor chatting up Lord Billows. Did you make any headway?"

"He wanted to put me up for a club," I said.

"Jolly good," Horton said.

"I told him I wasn't interested."

"That was pretty stupid," Sanger said. "He was trying to do you a favor."

I could tell from Horton's expression that he was in sympathy with Sanger's remark.

Sanger still faced me. I said, "So you approve of discrimination against people on the grounds of sex?"

"It's a London club," he said.

"They don't allow women to join."

Sanger said, "Are you afraid they'll turn you down?"

Horton and the others looked shocked, and Margaret Duboys said, "I don't want to get drawn into this discussion."

I said, "Tell me, Sanger, is that remark characteristic of your tact? Because if it is, I'd say your mouth is an even greater liability than your face."

"Gentlemen, please," Horton said, in his coach's voice. "Before this turns into a slanging match, can we move on to something less controversial? I need something on Mrs. Whiting—the second Mrs. Whiting. Did anyone have a word with her?"

Scaduto said, "I didn't get anywhere."

"She makes furniture," I said. "Very small furniture. For dollhouses."

Sanger said, "You dig deep."

"And cutlery," I said. "Very tiny forks and knives. If you wanted to stab someone in the back"—here I looked at Sanger—"I don't think you'd use one of Mrs. Whiting's knives."

Horton smiled. "Debbie wants her on a committee. We had no idea what her interests were. That's useful. What about our MPs?"

Jeeps said, "The finance bill passed with a government majority of sixteen. I've just had a phone call. There were eight abstentions."

"Good man," Horton said. "Were any of those abstentions ours?"

"Six Labour, two Liberal. The Tories were solid."

Miss Duboys said, "Derek Yarrow filled me in on the antinuclear lobby. It seems to be growing."

Jeeps said, "I did a number on Mrs. Yarrow."

"What did you make of Mr. Yarrow?" Horton asked me, and I realized that in spite of the crowded party my movements had been closely monitored.

"Blustery," I said. There was no agreement. "Contemptuous. Probably tricky."

"He's given us a lot of help," Sanger said.

"He seemed rather untrustworthy to me. He described his constituency as 'squalid.' I didn't like that."

"That's a snap judgment."

"Precisely what I felt," I said, and Sanger scowled at me for deliberately misunderstanding him. "He's a born-again Tory. He lectured me on Europe. You realize of course that he was a Communist."

"That's not news to us," Scaduto said.

"I intend to read his book," I said.

Sanger appeared to be speaking for the others when he said, "Yarrow doesn't write books."

"He wrote one. It didn't sell. It was political. Howlett published it."

"Yarrow's a heavy hitter," Sanger said.

"Thank you," I said, scribbling. "I collect examples of verbal kitsch."

Horton said, "Do me a memo on Yarrow's book after you've read it." Then, "Was Sophie Graveney alone?"

"Yes," Steve Kneedler said. It was his one offering and it was wrong.

"No," Jeeps said. "She left with the BBC guy—the one with the fake American accent. I think she lives with him."

"That would be Ramsay," Horton said.

"She doesn't live with Ramsay," I said.

"How do you know that?" Jeeps said.

I said, "Ramsay's address is given as Hampstead. Sophie Graveney doesn't live in Hampstead."

"Islington," Jeeps said. "It's not far."

"Then why is it," I said, "that she jogs around Battersea Park every morning?"

The others stared at me. Horton said, "Maybe you can put us in the picture. If she's living with someone there, we ought to know about it."

Scaduto said, "Her mother's Danish."

"So was Hamlet's," Sanger said.

"I've just realized what it is that I don't like about the English aristocracy," Scaduto said. "They're not English! They're Danes, they're Germans, they're Greeks, Russians, Italians. They're even Americans, like Lady Astor and Churchill's mother. They're not English! My charlady is more English than the average duke in his stately home. What a crazy country!"

Margaret Duboys said, "The Greeks royal family is Swedish," and this seemed to put an end to that subject.

But there was more. The guest list was gone through and each guest discussed so thoroughly that it was as if there had been no party but rather an occasion during which fifty British people had passed in review for us to assess them. Miss Duboys said that she had found out more on the Brownlow merger, and Jeeps said that he had more on his profile about the printing dispute at the *Times*, and Sanger said, "If anyone wants my notes on export licensing, I'll make a copy of my update. Tony Whiting gave me a few angles.

He's got a cousin in a Hong Kong bank."

I said, "No one has mentioned that fidgety white-haired fellow."

"Howlett," said Scaduto.

"No. I met Howlett," I said. "The one I'm talking about said his name was Edward Heaven. He wasn't on the guest list."

"Everyone was on the guest list," Horton said.

"Edward Heaven wasn't," I said.

No one had any idea who this man was; no one had spoken to him or indeed seen him. But there was no mystery. Before we left Briarcliff Lodge, Horton called the embassy and got the telex operator, a young fellow named Charlie Hogle. Hogle took the name Edward Heaven and had the duty officer run it through the computer. The reply came quickly. Two years previously, Edward Heaven had been Horton's florist. He was probably still associated with the florist and had found out about the party because of the flowers that had been delivered. Mr. Heaven had crashed the party. Horton said that he would now get a new florist and would try to tighten security. You couldn't be too careful, he said. They were kidnaping American diplomats in places like Paris.

"I think we can adjourn," he said, finally. "It's been a long day." At the door, he said, "You look tired, fella."

"I'm not used to working overtime," I said.

"You've been spoiled by the Far East," he said. "But you'll learn." He clapped me on the shoulder. "I know it's expecting a lot—after all, you're new here. But I like to start as I mean to go on."

Born and raised in Massachusetts, the observant and witty Paul Theroux now divides his time between London and Cape Cod. He writes short stories, novels, and non-fiction, and his international reputation continues to soar. He has won the Whitbread Award in England and an American Institute Award in Literature from the American Academy and Institute of Arts and Letters. Mr. Theroux's story "White Lies" appeared in SSI No. 34.

"Yaw'll kain't jest take her from me. You kain't!"

Cookie

BY MIGNON HOLLAND ANDERSON

LOOKING up, she went blind for a moment. The August sun had fused white and broiling with the sky. Nellie Harper lowered the withered hand which defended her eyes from the glare and trudged on, head down, along the beginning of a long row of tomato plants. Her shoes were soon clogged with field dust as she stepped carefully to find even footing. She was much too old to move between the hot powdery tomato rows with the ease of even three years before. Arthritis afflicted her right hip so that her walk was the heavy and labored toddle of a cripple, the painful slowness of her gait, one peculiar to the disease.

Cookie watched the old woman's approach with a deepening despair. She was only fourteen, so perhaps it was something ageless in her mind, coupled with the tough and violent struggle she had already experienced which caused her to see herself in Nellie as the old woman limped toward her.

Nellie was dark brown, just a little darker than Cookie, tired in her eyes and at the corners of her mouth. Her skin along face, neck and arms, sagged, as tired as her expression. She stopped every ten feet or so to rest. Each time, small clouds of dust settled over her feet and legs and formed delicate yellowish lines along the hem of her long dark blue skirt. The old woman shook her head wearily at the sun, murmured something under her breath, and started off again along the row.

Men, women and children, forty rows or so away, were bent low in the middle section of the field. Down on their knees, bushel baskets of tomatoes lined up beside them, rows of dust-covered Black folk leaned beneath the heat and picked for their lives, none of them aware of Cookie, who she was or where she had come from.

Some were home folk, people who had been born and reared on the lower Eastern Shore of Virginia, most of whom would probably never leave. They worked in a group by themselves. Others were migrants, up from Florida like Cookie, the temporary and shifting farm labor force of the Atlantic Seaboard. The old psychology was at work here. The migrants were the lowest on the white man's scale of worth. Poor home-grown Black people were one step up, and many of the home folk acted accordingly. There was practically no communication between the two groups, so Cookie turned back to her picking as the old woman drew close, not planning to speak and not expecting to be spoken to by one who probably considered herself to be superior.

Cookie leaned over the tomato basket just to her left as Nellie approached her from the right side. Her blouse was full and easily covered the basket, rim to rim, so that any view of its contents was obscured. Nellie painfully turned around a few steps past the girl and gave her a studied look. Cookie held her position, growing instantly nervous that the old woman had noticed something.

"You know," Nellie said. "Unda all that tomato fiel' dust, you'se got one of the pretties' faces I'se ever seen." Cookie looked up in surprise.

"What's yo' name, sugar?"

"Cookie," she said, resuming her work. She was careful to keep the basket between herself and Nellie.

"You looks hongry, Cookie," Nellie said. "You too thin. But you sho' is pretty. I'se Sis Harpa. Come lunch time, I'll be comin' back thisaway. I'll bring you somethin' real good for you' lunch. You hear?"

"Yes'm." Cookie smiled, struggling for a moment not to cry. Nellie returned her smile and limped on her way. Such a small kindness overwhelmed Cookie so that when she looked down into the basket at her four-month-old baby, tears dropped onto the baby's fingers, leaving brown spots where there had been a tan coating of dust.

Cookie watched after Nellie, off and on, as she made her way across the distance and finally disappeared among a line of tall juniper trees which marked the beginnings of a green lawn and a huge white house, but not before Nellie had looked back at the girl just short of a dozen times. She had seen herself in Cookie as clear as day, even though she hadn't seen that Cookie had a baby. She knew that as she had once been, Cookie was a prime candidate for abuse.

"Nobody loved me," Nellie whispered aloud, her mouth trembling for a second until it held tightly against her own feelings. "Nobody done nothing to he'p me, and being twelve, my baby died. A little boy. Looked like my baby brother what died. Not 'til I met Willie Pete did anybody give a damn 'bout me. An' I was growd by then. Sixty odd year and the same little gurl pickin' in the same dust on the groun'. Same little gurl." She had walked onto the neat green lawn in a state of grief and quandary.

The baby began to cry. She was loosely wrapped in an adult's faded blue cotton shirt, and was propped up on burlap padding inside the basket. Cookie stopped picking, wiped tomato stain from her hands against her dress and leaned over her baby, playing with its fingers as she forced a worried smile. She wondered how different life must be across that lawn in that big white house. Things were clean there and there was plenty to eat and new things to enjoy. She wondered if what the old woman had said was true; that she was pretty? She didn't ever remember feeling pretty. Where she had been and where she was going were nothing like what she imagined that pretty house to be.

Cookie cast her eyes down, depression filling her mind and body. She stared absently at the mucus bubbling from her baby's nose and reached into her pocket for a piece of coarse toilet paper stolen from the labor camp outhouse. She tore off a foot-long piece, folded it, and wiped at the baby's nose. The infant was terribly congested and try as she might, Cookie couldn't stop what became a seemingly endless thick yellowish flow. The baby choked and burst into loud and angry crying.

Cookie shifted quickly into a sitting position in the midst of an enveloping cloud of dust, picked up the baby, and made consoling sounds as she lowered the infant's face down over her thigh and patted her small back, wiping at her tiny nose as best she could all the while. She sneaked looks at the pickers way behind her, trying to see if any of them had heard the baby crying, but no one seemed to have noticed. After wiping and folding the tissue over several times, removing several heavy yellow clots, the baby seemed able to comfortably breathe again. Little Lyn suckled and sputtered, her nose partially clogged, stopped for breath and returned hungrily to the breast. Cookie rocked her gently, hummed a tune she vaguely remembered hearing nursing mothers hum and struggled to hold back tears of panic. Little Lyn was worse now than even an hour before, and Cookie knew it. She also knew nowhere to turn. She had learned, finally, on the afternoon when the conception of this baby was forced on her by her stepfather, that trusting anybody was a deadly mistake. For a moment she relived that awful afternoon in the bushes behind the labor camp where they had lived in Florida. For a moment she didn't hear Lyn choking, her nose once again closed with mucus.

Once again she wiped at the baby's nose, her little face contorted with annoyance at being pulled away from the breast. She cried a deep, angry cry, pawed at her mother's chest and blew another bubble from her nose as she struggled for breath. Cookie wound more tissue into a ball and stood up with Lyn, leaving her partially filled tomato baskets where they were. She had to get both of them out of the sun and the one place where there were trees was away from the direction of the camp and on the edge of the old woman's green lawn.

The junipers provided a fine spread of shade with the sun hovering just above the roof of the house behind the trees. Cookie dozed and held her baby and dreamed splintered pieces of nightmares while Lyn nursed her second course on Cookie's other side.

An unexpected voice startled Cookie from behind.

"Why you brought that baby out yhere in this heat?" Nellie's voice was hoarse and demanding, yet full of kindness. The girl looked into the old face as her baby lolled off into sleep.

"I lives in Mista Barnses camp. He ain't got no place fuh me to leave little Lyn whilst I works. She too young fuh to be alone, and I has to work...What you think?...I does the bes' I kin."

Nellie drew in her breath. "This yo' baby?" she said in sad realization. It was the same story being run into the ground again. "My goodness, Chil'. You'se jest a baby yo'se'f. You kain't be more'n twelve if you'se a day,"

"I'se fou'teen."

"Well, that's not much betta. You'se a baby. You'se both jest babies."

Little Lyn roused irritably from her sleep, her nose once again clogged. She coughed, spit and sputtered, crying pitifully at her inability to draw a clear breath. Nellie could hear the rawls as she breathed out through her open mouth.

Nellie bent down as best her old bones would allow and placed her palm of her hand against the baby's forehead.

"Lord, Chil', you' baby got a fever, honey. It needs a doctor as sure as I'm born. She need a doctor now. You grab that chil' up and follow me."

"You not gonna take my baby away. No you ain't." Cookie got to her feet, grabbed up her headrag which had fallen from her pocket and turned to leave.

"You know they's nothin' fuh you or yo' baby back thataway. She's sick, Chil'. Don't take much to kill a po' little baby. You come on wit' me. Dr. Conner is the onliest Black doctor on the whole Easton Sho'. He won't take you' baby away. I promise you that. But she got a fever. She's too hot to live if she don't get he'p.

You knows that, don't you. You yhear me?"

Cookie had started away, but Nellie's words found their place in her heart so that she stopped, turned around and followed the old woman, every step toward the big white house set down in fear.

All night she had prayed for help. She had only arrived in the camp a day before, and nobody much seemed friendly, maybe because she was afraid to let them be. The contractor had pointed out a small tin-roofed hut where she could spend the night, so she had gone where he said, afraid that if she asked questions, he would ask them of her and end up taking her to the authorities.

He had asked her about her age and she had lied. He had looked at her, up and down slowly, only his eyes moving, his tongue wetting his lips without a sound. She had sat awake most of the night holding the biggest stick she could find, thinking that in the dead of the night he would come and hurt her. She didn't know why he didn't come.

It was only now that it was beginning to dawn on her that Lyn might have more than just a summer cold. There had been no one to ask who looked the part of help or compassion. Even now, following this feeble old woman, Cookie expected and was resigned to the worst. Her common sense and mother's instinct ruled her now more than her very real fear of losing Lyn to the Welfare people. Lyn started to heave in her arms as they walked the last twenty yards to the back door of the house. Cookie held the baby out from her as hot sour milk shot out from Lyn's mouth and spurted with mucus through her nose onto the ground. Even face down, the baby seemed to be drowning in her own fluids. Lyn screamed in panic and looked to the old woman as she rushed back to them as fast as her age and arthritis would allow.

"You gimme the baby, Chil' and then you go in there and call Miz Conner to come outchere right away! Hurry now! Go right on in there and call Miz Conner!"

Cookie did as she was told. In seconds, Elizabeth Conner had the baby in her arms and was rushing across the side lawn to her husband's office.

Nellie had almost given out with all of the rushing about in the heat and had to be helped along by Cookie, who was more frightened than ever that she would never see her baby again.

The office was a beautiful place to Cookie, who had never in her life been inside a decent house. The walls were of mahogany and the chairs were a dark red leather. The carpet on the floor was deep and rich and cushioned her feet so well that she was afraid to walk on it. Her shoes on the rug, old sneakers, seemed to her a desecration. She looked down at the dark blue of it and halted just inside the door.

"Come on in, gurl. You come sit down and Doc Conner will take care of everthin'. He's a good doctor. Kin cure 'bout anythang."

Cookie looked around. The draperies were a pale blue with white birds delicately embroidered here and there in haphazard pattern. The room was air-conditioned so cool that it gave her chills, and the neatly dressed black lady in white behind the pretty wooden desk who was now standing, looking at Cookie, had a kind and concerned look to her.

"Cookie?" Nellie walked slowly back over to the girl and tugged at her arm, pulling her gently toward a chair. Once Cookie was settled, Nellie limped over to the receptionist, Mrs. Thompson, and spoke with her voice low.

"Dis here chile is hongry. Kin you go ast Miz Conner if they's gonna be long with the baby. If'n they is, I jest as well take Cookie back to the house for somethin' to eat. She jest a baby her ownself."

Mrs. Thompson nodded and disappeared through the examining room door. The baby's half-strangled cries blared suddenly through the door and sent Cookie to her feet and halfway into the next room before Nellie caught her from behind and Mrs. Thompson stopped her by barring her way.

"I jest wants to see little Lyn," Cookie sobbed. "She ain't never been wit' nobody but me. She's mines. Yaw'll kain't jest take her from me. You kain't!"

"She going to be fine, Miss. Please. You must wait in the waiting room. You just have to."

Mrs. Conner, hearing the commotion, directed Mrs. Thompson to take her place helping the doctor while she talked to Cookie.

She put her arm around the girl and walked with her to a chair where she sat Cookie down, drew up her own seat and leaned earnestly forward.

"Cookie, I'm Elizabeth Conner. My husband's the doctor who's in there with your baby." She patted Cookie's hand to reassure her and gazed at her steadily, doing all she could to help her to be calm and to understand.

Cookie looked back at Elizabeth through tears which clouded eyes coming to anger. This was a rich light-skinned lady who didn't know the first thing about her, she was thinking and on the verge of saying.

"Cookie, the baby has pneumonia."

"Oh, Lord," Cookie said, covering her mouth with her hands. "She's gonna die, ain't she? Or maybe you'se lying to me so's you can take her to the Welfare people."

Elizabeth shook her head. "The answer is no to both of those things. Your baby, with good care from all of us, should be well in a week or two. She's not going to die. And right now our only concern is getting both of you on your feet. We're not going to call anybody at Welfare."

Cookie looked to Nellie for assurance and received her nod. She wiped at the tears which had entirely wet her face, distrust in her eyes mixed with a fervent hope.

"Dr. Connor is giving her an antibiotic. We'll feed you both whatever you need and put you both to bed for awhile until you're well enough to decide what you want to do next. Does that sound all right?"

"Yes'm." Cookie sat back in the chair, trembling slightly from fatigue and worry and closed her eyes as tears flowed down her face. Nellie came with a cool wet cloth and tended Cookie while Elizabeth went back in for the baby. She and the doctor came back into the waiting room in just a few minutes with little Lyn newly diapered and wrapped in a light blanket. Elizabeth placed the baby in Cookie's arms and while the little girl rocked her infant and cried over her in relief, Tom and Elizabeth Conner took a deep breath and shared a look which spoke silently of a shared understanding.

That evening with Cookie and little Lyn finally asleep upstairs in a large bed which sat by a picture window in a little girl's room, Tom and Elizabeth sat at their kitchen table drinking coffee, a sense of peace and excitement inside of them like none they had known in well over ten years. That bedroom had been empty, unused by anyone all that time, left vacant by a daughter who had drowned toward the end of a hot summer's day. They had thought they couldn't have another child. Elizabeth was forty-eight. They had thought they would have no more children ever cross their threshold. They simply hadn't thought enough. But that had changed in the twinkling of a moment of mutual need, unpretentious and blinding in its clarity, when Ms. Nellie Harper had told them of the beautiful little girl in the tomato field as they had had their breakfast. The thinking had begun, set in motion by their need and an old woman's pain over a migrant, outcast, lost child, as Nellie once had been, who dearly needed a bed, a room, a home.

Born in Virginia, Mignon Holland Anderson received a BA at Fisk University and a MFA at Columbia University. She and her two children now live in a suburb of Washington, D.C. Her short stories are published in literary journals. She has written several novels. All her work expresses her concern with the internal struggles and growth of Black Americans. Her story "Boots" appeared in SSI No. 39.

"My mother is worried that my father's and our ancestors' souls can't find their way here."

Integration

BY UYEN LOEWALD

SUSAN, a teacher of immigrants, has a special regard for her Vietnamese refugee students; they have hardly recovered from the shock of leaving their homeland and being robbed at sea, but already they've become achievers. It is difficult for her not to feel they're special. Unlike the Mexicans who live next door to the United States, or many native Americans, the Vietnamese take advantage of every free service; community colleges are full of Vietnamese students. The number of Vietnamese seeking welfare keeps dropping daily. Maybe it is their culture; maybe it is their natural industry. Whatever motivates them, Susan would like to know about it. She wants to know why old Vietnamese women who can no longer enter the work force, who have children to interpret for them, keep coming to school night after night to learn English.

The Vietnamese surprised many people by not wanting to do physical work and being keen on intellectual challenges; they have won prizes in several fields. Electronics firms in San Jose are full of them. Susan can understand that: they know they cannot compete against American six-footers so they turn to areas where they have special skills.

If Susan could discover what makes women like Mrs. Ba persist in learning English, she would be able to help other minorities who are still reluctant to integrate. Vietnamese people do not form ghettos. That surely must help them progress.

Mrs. Ba does not need to learn English; she lives with two well-educated sons: an engineer and a doctor; both are devoted to her. They speak English without any trace of an accent. The engineer is exceptionally brilliant; he has become an architect since he arrived and has won a national prize.

Maybe deprivation sharpens keenness. Mrs. Ba told her, in her broken English, that she had never gone to school before she left Vietnam. Maybe if state governments forbid minorities from attending schools, the way they forbid drugs, it would spur them to learn. Americans take too much for granted, the Vietnamese have often told her that.

Susan is excited about having dinner at Mrs. Ba's house; she worked hard for the invitation. But she thinks she'll tell the sixty-five year old woman not to come to class any more. There are such things as failing teachers and hindering age. Mrs. Ba could catch pneumonia one day; she is not used to cold weather. And her persistence has been sapping Susan's patience.

There is so much Susan wants to know about Confucian society and about extended families. She can ask Mrs. Ba's sons everything; then she won't see Mrs. Ba's contortions as she curls her tongue trying to pronounce the "w" and "th" sounds; it always pains her to see Mrs. Ba's distorted face. Susan has often wanted to comfort Mrs. Ba, to pat her hand and tell her not to come to class; her sons can interpret for her. There is no need for her to go out, particularly on windy and rainy days, when her already pale face turns bloodless and her teeth chatter. But body contact is forbidden in the East. Or do Vietnamese conventions and habits give way in integration? Mrs. Ba looked lost that time when she tried to shake hands with Susan. Her hands looked as if they had suddenly become detached from her body.

Susan briefly saw the inside of Mrs. Ba's home only once, on a rainy day, when Mrs. Ba had a fever and could not go home by bus. Shyly, Mrs. Ba had accepted Susan's offer of a ride home. It had been interesting to see how Mrs. Ba sat at the edge of the car seat, her face turned away, her body drawn tight to avoid Susan's dog, who tried to lick her.

It took Susan a while to understand that teachers command absolute respect in Confucian societies, just as parents do. That's why Mrs. Ba hadn't asked Susan to visit her at home, although she never failed to bring her presents for Christmas, her birthday, and the Vietnamese New Year. The ability to progress while retaining their own culture is their key to successful integration. It is an outstanding Vietnamese quality.

As she parks her car in front of Mrs. Ba's home, behind two new Honda Preludes next to their neat lawn, Susan realizes she's hungry. There is no indication that the occupants of the house are relatively recent arrivals in the country. Only the smell of incense as the door opens and Mrs. Ba's dark silk *ao-dai* make the house different.

"Miss Susan, please come in," Mrs. Ba joins her hands and smiles as she leads Susan to the living room. Long stemmed red roses are arranged beautifully in a crystal vase in the middle of a large glass-top coffee table. A modern sofa and four chairs match the color and design of the Danish dining set in front of the wide glass sliding door leading to the courtyard which has orchids in full bloom growing on all sides. A chest against the wall facing the sun is the altar, displaying a round tray of steaming food, a vase of white lilies, miniature glasses half-filled with rice wine, an open decanter, a tray of paper money, rice cake, fancy French assorted biscuits and tropical fruit. The incense is burning.

Susan shyly hands her gift to Mrs. Ba. "I hope I didn't do the wrong thing," she says.

Mrs. Ba chooses to relax instead of practicing English. Her handsome son, who looks like a well-behaved teen-ager, says, "You have done the right thing by bringing a present; our New Year is like Christmas; people exchange gifts. But you should know that most Vietnamese don't like chocolate or cheese. But we are learning." His smile feels like a caress; it makes her self-conscious.

She sees there are four places set at the table. Mrs. Ba's children must be single.

"This house is too big for three people. My sons have to find wives as soon as possible." Mrs. Ba looks proud after her long sentence.

Susan blushes. Could it be an invitation? They are integrated.

"My mother told us to get married as soon as we arrived here. We did not marry in Vietnam because we did not want our children to be victims of the war. My mother has been reminding us ever since." The doctor laughs. "She doesn't want us to be lonely; she wants grandchildren."

The architect says something in Vietnamese. Mrs. Ba springs up, goes to the altar, bends to make four deep bows, then three light ones. She says something in Vietnamese. Her sons remove the food from the altar.

"Now you can see how we Vietnamese blend culture with technology; we heat shark fin and fish bladder soup in the microwave oven." The doctor holds the tray as his brother loads the large microwave oven in the corner near the dining table and under the shelf displaying Vietnamese artifacts.

Susan notices the landscape paintings on the walls. She admires the lacquerware panels inlaid with mother-of-pearl; they are skillfully carved into the gentle shapes of autumn leaves and spring flowers.

"These are the scenery of four seasons," the architect says, looking at his mother. "I was too young when we left the North, so I only know one season. In Saigon, it's hot all year round. In Vietnam, only rich people can afford those things. We were too poor."

Susan likes his honesty, but she feels uncomfortable when he looks so intently at her. She moves to the picture on the altar. She can see the resemblance between the handsome man in that picture and Mrs. Ba's children.

"This is my husband." Mrs. Ba frowns. She must have been a beautiful woman once, when her teeth were intact. She wipes her eyes. "The Communists killed him. He never did anything to them. He did nothing harmful to anyone. They killed my daughter and son-in-law, too. He was an American." Mrs. Ba weeps.

The architect says something in Vietnamese to his mother, then turns to Susan. "According to Vietnamese custom, we must not think of anything sad today because whatever we do on the first day of the year will happen during the rest of the year. My father was killed in 1968, during the Tet offensive. You must have read about it."

The doctor adds, "The Vietcong almost took over Saigon, Hue and many other cities."

The microwave oven bell breaks the awkward silence. Mrs. Ba leads Susan to the dining table as her sons serve. She pulls her *ao-dai* to place its back panel on her lap, but she stands up again to take over the cutting of the rice cake with red chopsticks. They help Susan with soup and pork pâté. Mrs. Ba says something in Vietnamese, then the doctor explains: "Red is lucky; yellow is royal, used to be anyway, used to be forbidden too, when we still had an emperor. Chinese people wrap money in red paper, to give to children during the New Year. That's why we use red chopsticks. During the rest of the year, we just use ordinary bamboo or plastic ones." He removes the bowls which were used for soup, then distributes clean ones as Mrs. Ba puts pieces of pork pâté and cinnamon pork into her bowl.

Susan asks: "How long did it take you to prepare all this?"

Mrs. Ba smiles and the architect answers. "My mother did everything yesterday. In Vietnam, Tet is celebrated for at least a week. Special kinds of foods are prepared so that during that period people don't have to work. Rice cake keeps for two weeks. When you feel hungry, you just cut a piece and eat. Fish stewed in tea also keeps well. It is made of the cheapest kind of fish and when all its flesh has been eaten, its bones and spices are stewed with pickled cabbage. People eat the lot. Pork pâté and pork cinnamon are prepared in the same way. The paste used to take a strong man hours to make. But the food processor has simplified everything. My mother made this in a matter of minutes." He offers her jellyfish salad. "This dish used to take women all day to make: carrots, cucumbers, everything had to be shredded by hand as thin as possible, the thinner they are, the better the chance for the maiden to get married. It's part of the *Four Virtues*. Japanese invention has simplified the maidens' tasks. Even I can make it in half an hour. But the maidens need not worry; there is a shortage of Vietnamese women among refugees."

His eyes make Susan feel self-conscious again. But his gestures remove her disgust from eating jellyfish. It tastes like a delicious crisp salad with a rich yet delicate flavor. Its color is superb: red, green, yellow, white, all mingled together.

Mrs. Ba eats like a sparrow. To Susan she says, "Please, have some more," and she loads her bowl again. There is something about Mrs. Ba which makes Susan feel protected, nurtured.

Now Susan feels sufficiently comfortable to say: "Please tell me why Vietnamese people are so keen to learn English. Why you are so keen when you don't really need to learn? You are the most studious person in my class."

"Learning is difficult for me." Tears return to Mrs. Ba's eyes.

The doctor gives her a box of tissues as he says: "My mother is worried that my father's and our ancestors' souls can't find their way here; they may be wandering, homeless, and hungry. That's why she goes to school every day by bus to learn English. She wants to know the map of the city and speak English well, so when she dies, her soul can go back to Vietnam and bring theirs here with her. Knowing English will also help her understand her grandchildren when they call her soul back on her death anniversary. She has known many Vietnamese children who cannot speak Vietnamese. And she is not sure that we are going to marry Vietnamese wives!"

Born in 1940, in Haiduong (near Hanoi), Uyen Loewald went to South Vietnam in 1951. She was a student of literature and mathematics in Saigon. In 1962 she was imprisoned by the Diem regime. She is currently in Australia. Her story "Victory" appeared in SSI No. 75.

"He turned his back to me in absolute fury
and went away mumbling like a bear..."

Door Handle

BY FADIL HADZICH

IN the first days of this year I opened the door of the living room
and the door handle remained in my hand.

I went to the locksmith and asked him to come and fasten the
door handle. The locksmith, greasy and unshaven, scribbled
something in his notebook and said he would come the following
day around noon. I waited for him but he did not show up. I visited
him again.

"Hadn't you said you would repair my door handle yesterday?"

"I'm going to be there today!" the locksmith promised patting
me on the shoulders heartily.

It was a sign of attachment, since locksmiths don't tap
everybody on the shoulders—only those from their neighboring
streets. I waited for the whole afternoon, but he did not come.
Together with my wife I went away for the weekend and first thing
on Monday, I ran to the locksmith.

"Well, where've you been?" the locksmith greeted me.

"I waited for you the whole day!" I answered humbly, because the locksmith looked at me in a way which did not promise much.

"We came there a day later and rang your doorbell for half an hour!" the locksmith said sharply.

"We were away for the weekend..."

"And what can we do now?" the locksmith stared at my feet apathetically as I was shifting them nervously in place.

"Please, come with me right away. Let's go together, so there won't be any misunderstanding," I suggested, grasping his biceps chummily.

"All right. I just have to stop by a lady's place in the neighborhood and then I'm going to visit you!" the locksmith agreed and began to pack the tools into his black bag.

I waited from ten in the morning till midnight—he did not show up. The following day he awaited me angrily: "So, what was the matter with you this time?"

"What do you mean, what's the matter with me? I waited for you for fourteen hours!"

"And what do you think I was doing? Playing dominoes?" snarled the locksmith at me and raised his eyebrows as if speaking to his apprentice.

"I don't get it," I replied sincerely and meekly.

"I don't get it either. I rang your doorbell at least ten times, and you were supposedly waiting for me!" the locksmith stared at me suspiciously and fixedly.

"Where did you ring?"

"At your door on the third floor."

"I live on the ground floor."

"Since when?"

"Since at least ten years ago."

"Your name is Mushitza?"

"No, my name is Hadzic, and Musica lives on the third floor."

"Holy Virgin Mary," the locksmith cussed through his yellow teeth, "then I rang the wrong bell!"

"Let's make an appointment," I suggested desperately. "Come today at one."

"I can't! I could tomorrow at one," concluded the locksmith and again tapped me on the shoulders, which meant that he'd forgiven me this misunderstanding.

The following day at one I prepared coffee and domestic slivovitz for him, and waited till ten in the evening, biting my fingernails. Mad as a rabid dog I went to the locksmith the day after, and noticed a note on the door—"Be back immediately." I came back seven times, but the note—"Be back immediately"—remained untouched. The day after it was still in the same place, and on the third day I learned from the neighboring barber that the locksmith had gone to the seacoast.

He came back fresh and tan. His round belly was leaping like a young thoroughbred.

"Have you ever had grilled squid?" he welcomed me from the doorway.

"Haven't."

"That's something divine, but only if you wash it down with good red wine."

I reminded him about my door handle timidly and passed over my waiting in silence, fearing that I might spoil his religious experience with grilled squid.

"We'll see to it at once. Let me just quickly drop by these people on that side of the road—some demon clogs their waterpipe so it's been flooding there all night long." He pointed out a house with tenants waving their arms like passengers on a wrecked ship.

I admitted to myself that one door handle, compared to a *Deluge*, was after all a trivial matter.

"I'll be at your place in half an hour at the latest!" promised the locksmith with the zest of a man who has had his fill of sea food specialties and now has enough strength to please the whole of humanity.

I waited for two days, I had already decided to go to another locksmith, but I ran into the selfsame one in the streets.

"Have you repaired that door handle of yours?" he asked me absent-mindedly, like a prof·ssor who doesn't know where he forgot his umbrella.

"I haven't yet," I mumbled in a far from friendly manner.

"Well, then wait for me at home, I'll be there in ten minutes." He patted me heartily on my shoulder and went into a tavern from which a small party of cheerful citizens waved to him.

I watched from the window to see him come out. It was nighttime when the tavern closed and he barely managed to cross the street and sit in his car. I prayed the Lord he would not try to visit me because in this state he might take the whole night to repair the door handle.

Two days later I entered his workshop with my head bowed, as if in a church, and asked him to settle the question of my door handle in a friendly way once for all.

"I've had it with these little gadgets," said the locksmith aggressively, and added more calmly: "I'd do it for nobody else except you; a door handle is not worth the effort of walking."

He promised he would come on Thursday; I waited the whole morning, but he did not come.

That same evening we had guests for dinner and I was ashamed in front of all the guests that the door of the living room, where they were received, had no handle. A small thing, but a bother even on a pigsty door.

A guest, an engineer, noticed during the meal that there was no door handle, and offered to repair it. He took a piece of thick wire, rasped it with a file somehow, and in no more than ten minutes the handle glistened on the door. I could not believe my eyes. We opened a bottle of an imported champagne, which I had kept for two years, to celebrate.

At dawn the following morning the locksmith appeared at the door. He stood dignified and self-confident, like a man who's doing a favor for me. He carried his black tool-bag the way an ambassador hands a portfolio of agreements to the President of a country.

I explained to him that the door handle had been repaired.

"Listen, Mr. Hadzic," he gruntled angrily, "I have no time to waste! You beg me to come, and then you give the job to somebody else."

I could not explain it to him. He turned his back to me in absolute fury and went away mumbling like a bear and spitting on the walls.

It ended well. He could have applied his tools to my head.

This is Fadil Hadzich's first story to be published in English. A very pleasant person, he is a major Yugoslav writer, well-known in Eastern Europe and the USSR. He has written several collections of short stories and a number of novels and screenplays. He has also written and produced a dozen plays. His translator, Josip Novakovich, immigrated to the USA thirteen years ago. Mr. Novakovich is himself a published short story writer.

The Perfect Gift...
for all ocasions.

First gift (or your own) $22, all other gifts $20 each.

Where in the world can you find a gift like *SSI*? It is a gift that keeps on giving all year long, a gift that takes you to all points of the compass, to anywhere in the world. There are intriguing stories waiting for you in future issues of *SSI*—stories that will involve you in corners of the world you've never seen...and in worlds outside of this one...with fascinating glimpses into the future as well as the past.

Give a friend—relative—or yourself a year's subscription (6 issues) to *Short Story International*. The coupon below may be used for entering your own subscription and for giving a gift to impress and please. Every other month *SSI* will bring to you, and whomever you designate, the finest short stories gleaned from all the world—the mark of today's creative writers. Very few gifts could be more giving, more appropriate than *SSI*.

Order the first subscription, either your own or a gift, at the regular price of $22. Each additional subscription ordered at the same time is only $20. (This offer is good in U.S. and U.S. Possessions only and expires February 15, 1991.) Gift cards will be sent with your greetings.

A Harvest of the World's
Best Contemporary Writing Selected
and Published Every Other Month

Please enter my subscription to
Short Story International
P.O. Box 405, Great Neck, New York 11022
Six Issues for $22, U.S. & U.S. Possessions
Canada $24 (US), All Other Countries $25 (US)

Enclosed is my check for $_____ for _____ subscriptions.

Name _____

Address _____

City _____ State _____ Zip _____

Country _____

Please check   ☐ New Subscription   ☐ Renewal

Gift for:
Name _____
Address _____
City _____ State _____ Zip _____
Country _____
Please check ☐ New Subscription   ☐ Renewal

Gift for:
Name _____
Address _____
City _____ State _____ Zip _____
Country _____
Please check ☐ New Subscription   ☐ Renewal

Gift for:
Name _____
Address _____
City _____ State _____ Zip _____
Country _____
Please check ☐ New Subscription   ☐ Renewal

Gift for:
Name _____
Address _____
City _____ State _____ Zip _____
Country _____
Please check ☐ New Subscription   ☐ Renewal

Gift for:
Name _____
Address _____
City _____ State _____ Zip _____
Country _____
Please check ☐ New Subscription   ☐ Renewal

Gift for:
Name _____
Address _____
City _____ State _____ Zip _____
Country _____
Please check ☐ New Subscription   ☐ Renewal

For the young people in your life. . .

The world of the short story for young people is inviting, exciting, rich in culture and tradition of near and far corners of the earth. *You* hold the key to this world. . .a world you can unlock for the young in your life. . .and inspire in them a genuine love for reading. We can think of few things which will give them as much lifelong pleasure as the habit of reading.

Seedling Series is directed to elementary readers (grades 4-7), and **Student Series** is geared to junior and senior high school readers.

Our stories from all lands are carefully selected to promote and strengthen the reading habit.

Give a Harvest of the World's Best Short Stories
Published Four Times a Year for Growing Minds.

Please enter subscription(s) to:

____ **Seedling Series: Short Story International**
$14. U.S. & U.S. Possessions
Canada $17 (U.S.) All Other Countries $19 (U.S.)

____ **Student Series: Short Story International**
$16. U.S. & U.S. Possessions
Canada $19 (U.S.) All Other Countries $21 (U.S.)

Mail with check to:
Short Story International
P.O. Box 405, Great Neck, N.Y. 11022

Donor: Name _____
Address _____
City _____State_____Zip_____
Country _____

Send to: Name _____
Address _____
City _____State_____Zip_____
Country _____
Please check ☐ New Subscription   ☐ Renewal

Send to: Name _____
Address _____
City _____State_____Zip_____
Country _____
Please check ☐ New Subscription   ☐ Renewal